Ghosts of the Past
—& MURDER—

SHIRLEY GLOSTER

Printed in Canada

ISBN: 978-1-4866-1448-6

Word Alive Press
131 Cordite Road, Winnipeg, MB R3W 1S1
www.wordalivepress.ca

MIX
Paper from
responsible sources
FSC
www.fsc.org   FSC® C016245

Library and Archives Canada Cataloguing in Publication

Gloster, Shirley, author
      Ghosts of the past & murder / Shirley Gloster.

Issued in print and electronic formats.
ISBN 978-1-4866-1448-6 (softcover).--ISBN 978-1-4866-1449-3 (ebook)

      I. Title. II. Title: Ghosts of the past and murder.

PS8613.L675L46 2017   C813'.6   C2017-901470-6
                                              C2017-901471-4

*To my wonderful husband Bob, who always encouraged
my writing and my imagination. I know he is at home with
the Lord and would be so happy for me now.*

ACKNOWLEDGEMENTS

I would like to thank Sylvia St. Cyr of Word Alive Press, for making my dream come true; my newfound friend, editor Evan Braun, who is amazing and patient beyond words; my daughter Suzanne, for her encouragement and proofreading before I sent off the book to my editor; my two sons, Charles and David, for standing with me; and my late sister Lenore, who spent hours with her law experience helping me.

A very special thanks to my grandson, Daniel Robertson, for his computer knowledge where I need it. That is mind-boggling to me. Finally, but most importantly, I thank my God, who answers my prayers through faith. In his time, all things are possible.

CHAPTER ONE
THE LETTER

June 1993

Alexandria Rutherford was a reporter for a newspaper in Oakville, a good-sized tourist town on beautiful Lake Ontario, not far from Toronto. She came into work early in the morning all set for whatever the day might bring, anticipating getting a lead to an exciting story. These days there was always something going on, in spite of the statistics that said crime was down.

At five-foot-nine, Alex was barely aware of the admiration in both women and men as she passed them. Her tall slender figure and hair, dyed three shades of blond, fell attractively on her shoulders in soft curls. Her expressive dark blue eyes lent a probing quality to her features. Freckles claimed some space as well.

She knew how to dress casually yet smart. While she had an eye for fashion, it wasn't the most important thing in her life. Her mother had always been very fashion-conscious, and some of that had rubbed off on her.

Just inside the door of her department was the mail cubicle where everyone had a slot, and she always headed there first thing in the morning. When she looked into her slot, she saw several envelopes, including some junk mail. She tossed a handful into the garbage bin. Then she looked at each envelope she'd decided to keep.

One letter took her fancy. It had her name on it and the newspaper's address in bold handwriting. Did she recognize the writing? It did look sort of familiar, but she had witnessed lots of handwriting. She opened it out of curiosity and scanned its contents. Her brow furrowed. Then she leaned against the wall and read it again, not believing what she had read. The words "whole family" and "killer never found" caught her attention. There was even a mention that Alex's own family might be involved, sending shivers up her spine.

This can't be real, she thought, her body going hot and cold. She even entertained the possibility that it might not be real. It could just be some jerk wanting to gain notoriety. But if this were true, it would be the granddaddy of all stories.

She made her way to her own little cubbyhole of an office and laid the letter face-up on her desk. She then looked through the rest of the mail. Between each piece, her eyes drifted to the letter to her left. Nothing special about the paper or the envelope.

Despite the letter's intrigue, however, she opened a list of story assignments that her boss James wanted his reporters to look into. She found nothing as interesting as the letter.

Alex couldn't hold back the excitement any longer. If what the letter's author had written was true, if he or she had really killed a whole family a few years back, it had to have been reported someplace. No one could kill a whole family and it not be mentioned in the news somewhere. And if this story really did have something to do with Alex's family, it more than likely had happened in Haldimand County, or maybe Pelham. She loved that part of the country.

Alex spent half the day looking into anything that could prove even a hint of what the letter claimed. At first, she found nothing.

That's when an old wedding announcement caught her attention:

```
Lila Stratsfield and
Allen Williams were
married in Murphy
United Church on
May 3, 1958.
```

She had no idea if this had any bearing on the letter, but the letter had said that the name of the murdered family was Williams—and Alex's mother's maiden name was Stratsfield. She was excited, disappointed at the same time that she hadn't been able to find anything more.

Just when she was about to give up, she discovered a newspaper article about the police investigating a call about a family that may have been murdered in a house in the country. Alex looked into it only to read that the family had simply moved away. That agreed with what the letter claimed many people believed.

It wasn't much to go on. She looked through the same newspaper's archives and didn't find another word of it anywhere.

Was this just some weirdo with nothing better to do than write letters to send reporters on wild goose chases? Something wasn't right. Alex's senses started to stir, and the excitement she'd been trying to keep low-key gained ground again. One didn't just let a story like this go if it were real. The problem was, how could she prove it was real?

Suppose I decide to go after this story, she thought. *There's another problem. I'll have to convince James. He won't send me to cover it unless he's going to get something back. Another issue: going out of town comes with costs.*

She sighed, thinking he would never go for it. A forlorn expression crossed her face.

The letter occupied her thoughts for the rest of the day. That evening, she headed home and picked up Spider from the dog-sitter. Every morning, she dropped him off with a dear older lady, Mrs. Klighter, who had a huge, fenced-in back yard for him to run and play in. Alex paid the woman under the table to offset her meager pension.

Spider was waiting the minute Alex knocked on the door. As they cuddled, she once again noticed the unusual shape formed by a splotch of black hair on the back of the dog's neck. The pattern looked just like a spider, which is how he'd gotten his name.

After thanking Mrs. Klighter, they got in Alex's Suburban and headed home.

Alex looked into Spider's expressive brown eyes. "I have to tell you something, Spider." She explained to him all about the letter, as though hoping he would be able to give her the answer she so badly needed. "You have to admit that it isn't often one gets a letter like that in the mail. Should I take it seriously?"

Spider looked up at her as though he understood every word. It certainly wasn't the first time she'd shared her troubles with him. She sighed and the dog whimpered.

The trouble was that the writer of Alex's letter had added a few facts he or she must have known would draw her interest in particular. The writer had claimed that the victims were Alex's own relatives, cousins whom her family never spoke about. That alone was ridiculous.

"Every family has skeletons in their closet," she said aloud as she weaved through the heavy traffic.

She had memorized almost every word of the letter, and it wouldn't leave her mind. Reading it so many times in the past few hours made her want to investigate its possibilities all the more.

She rubbed the dog's ear. He let out a couple of short barks, as if he was trying to tell her something. Spider always seemed to know when she was upset or had something on her mind, and a few barks usually reassured her that everything was going to be all right.

"It's okay," she said. She wished he could give her some advice, but of course that was silly. "I just don't know what to do. I've talked to the Lord about it. Sometimes he shows me a picture, but I just don't get it. It's not the Lord's fault that I'm a little dense at times. That may be the case here."

Spider's wagging tail hit her arm. She smiled.

Alex had gone off to university in Toronto, not so far from home, and graduated with a degree in journalism. It was hard to believe that something so tragic could have happened to her family while she was gone. She would have been almost twenty...

She sighed. "That's hard to believe too. Where has the time gone? And why wouldn't I have known if something this horrid happened to my own cousins? It makes no sense. Maybe the family did just move away. The letter writer knows I have no way of contacting him, so what should I do, Spider?"

At the sound of his name, Spider lifted his head and rested it on her shoulder. Again he got his ear rubbed.

"Too bad you can't talk," Alex said.

She had been chasing stories for what seemed like forever. It was in her blood. When a story was in the making, investigating it gave her a feeling of gung-ho excitement from her head to her toes. She didn't want to feel like she had to pursue this particular story just because of family connections, but she had to be honest with herself: those connections made her want to pursue it even more. But even if this turned out to have nothing to do with her family, she would still have to learn the truth. If there was a real killer loose, she had to do something about it.

She just hated to think she was wasting her time.

"I don't dare go to James with what I have. I need more than just the letter, especially since I'd need the newspaper to cover my expenses for a couple of weeks."

Well, I have two weeks of holidays coming this month, she thought. *Maybe I can do both at the same time.*

Alex smiled, realizing that she'd made up her mind.

"Do you know what I'm going to do, Spider? I'm going to call my parents. You remember our last trip out to Niagara, how beautiful the falls are?"

She had been home for Easter and wished she'd had the letter then.

Alex pulled into her driveway and parked the Suburban. The house was located in an older, but still nice area of the Oakville. Her grandmother had left it to her when she died. Like a lot of homes in the area, it now had three apartments and she rented two of them to help pay the bills.

Once they had made their way into the house, she let Spider out into the back yard. She then changed into old ragged jeans and a comfy T-shirt. She loved being in her bare feet at home.

After she had eaten, she decided to call her parents. She heard the ringing and waited—and waited.

Her parents, Jessica and Stanley Rutherford, lived in Niagara Falls, a beautiful city. She had hated to leave home, yet she'd had to make them see she wasn't a kid any longer. She had decided to go to the big city, but she had ended up in Oakville instead, a decision she never regretted. It was all about growing up and becoming her own person.

"Hello," a woman's voice answered.

"Hi Mom, it's Alex calling. How are you today?"

"I'm fine, dear. Why are you calling so late in the evening? Is something wrong? Are you all right? Mind you, I'm always happy to hear your voice."

"Yes, Mom, everything is fine," she said. "I've come upon a story that has something to do with our area. Even weirder, it may even have a connection to our family. I was wondering, do you know of any relatives by the name of Williams? I seem to remember cousins with that name when I was a kid, but I'm not sure. Something about suddenly just moving away. It would have been about fifteen years ago."

Alex heard only a long silence. She listened, waiting for an answer. She was about to repeat the question when her mom finally spoke.

"What in the world are you talking about?"

"Well, it's kind of weird. Reporters often get strange letters from people claiming to know something. I received a letter that talks about some family that was murdered and whose bodies were never found. How they know the family was murdered, I don't know. It's so weird. Apparently the killer was never found either. The writer mentions that the victims might have been my relatives, so I was curious."

"My goodness, how ridiculous," her mom said. "My sister married a chap by the name of Williams. I'm surprised you don't remember, but then you were young and we had little to do with them. They moved away. I'm sure it must just be someone looking for publicity. I would ignore it. Some people like to prey on others for whatever reason. They have sick minds, but you should know that better than anyone. Please, dear, just forget it."

On the other side of the line, Jessica's heart beat faster. Her stomach threatened to give up its lunch. All that craziness with her sister Lila's family had happened fifteen years ago, just like her daughter had said. She still remembered the last time she'd seen her sister.

She nearly groaned out loud. Who would write a letter to Alex, of all people?

"The strange thing, Mom," Alex continued, "is that the letter writer wants me to investigate a cemetery in the country, near Canborough. If I remember right, we have some relatives buried out that way, don't we? I just thought it was odd. It's a fair way from Oakville, so for him to write me instead of someone closer... well, that also seems weird."

"You're right," Jessica confirmed. "We do have several relatives buried there, going back a good many years. Anyone from around here knows that. I even have your father looking into our family history, going from cemetery to cemetery getting information. We intend to put it into a book one day." She paused and drew a great breath. "By the way, summer's here. Are you coming home for a couple of weeks? What are your plans?"

"I'm not sure yet. But as far as I know, I'll be home. I also have some time coming up at the end of August, into September. I want to make a trip to Ottawa to spend time with my friend Shelly too."

Alex went on talking a few minutes more, and she even had a few words with her father.

"I have to go," she finally said. "Love you. Bye."

Alex ended the call and sat looking at the phone, not sure what to think. Dare she read into that conversation that the letter writer had been correct, and that her mother just didn't want to talk about it? All families had their secrets. Alex had forgotten all about her Williams cousins, and she couldn't remember much about them. They certainly hadn't been close.

After the call, Alex found herself even more raring to go.

She had made a few errors in her young life, some of them huge mistakes, and always because she hadn't listened to what the Lord was telling her. Upon leaving university, Alex had pursued jobs at three top news agencies, one a newspaper and the other two television stations. She had gone for interviews at each one and all had offered her a position. She had prayed, asking God for direction. She really needed him to be clear, as she had sometimes struggled with hearing him.

Give me a shove in the right direction, she had asked at the time. *Please Lord.*

"Trust in the Lord with all your heart, and lean not on your own understanding; in all your ways acknowledge Him, and He shall direct your paths."[1] She had learned that verse in Sunday school years ago and never forgot it. The book of Proverbs always held thoughts and answers for today.

She had chosen to work at the newspaper, believing that was what God wanted for her. She had been impressed with the editor and head honcho, James. She had really liked him. He'd told her that if she was any good, there was no limit as to what she could do.

That had been just what she wanted to hear, and she'd been working for him ever since. She loved the excitement of getting tips and following leads. She always seemed to have her eye on a story.

Alex looked down at Spider, fast asleep at her feet and snoring ever so slightly. She loved her dog. He was family to her, protective yet sociable too.

With her mind in such a jumble, Alex took a few minutes to talk to God. Prayer was a very important part of her life. Some of her friends didn't think being a crime reporter was a good job for a Christian, but Alex didn't think that was a fair evaluation. Some Christians thought they could do no wrong and walked around with a make-believe halo over their heads. Others never did anything wrong in their minds because they were Christians; for them, the name said it all. Still others were just ordinary, like her. She wasn't crazy religious, just one of those born-again Christians who was considered a little wacky.

---

[1] Proverbs 3:5–6.

Alex finished her prayer time and then went to sleep. Spider slept at the foot of the bed, taking up a lot of room.

CHAPTER TWO
WHAT TO DO?

The alarm woke her up. She sighed and made her way out of bed, the dog doing exactly the same thing; Spider was no more eager to get up than she was. She went through her usual routine, spending a little time with her Bible and then praying for God's guidance for the day. Once that was done, she got ready for work.

She fed Spider, let him out for his morning duty to perform, and then played with him for a while. That was their time together. She hated to leave him, but Mrs. Klighter lived quite close to work, and she loved Spider too.

Alex did have one indulgence: she always stopped at a drive thru and bought breakfast. Fortunately it never added any weight to her tall, slender frame. She spent two hours three times a week at a nearby gym, keeping fit. She liked the stair climbers best; they really burned the calories.

She finally arrived at work and set her briefcase on the small desk in her cubicle. She sat down, knowing what she wanted to do but not sure if it would be a waste of time or not. She read the letter again. Every time she did, even though she knew the words by heart, adrenalin raised through her body.

June 17, 1993

Ms. Alexandria Rutherford,

I'm not at liberty to tell you who I am, only to give you some facts. I believe you are a top-notch reporter. I recently discovered quite by accident in Melick Cemetery, just outside the village of Canborough, seven shallow graves. I believe they may belong to the Williams family.

Fifteen years ago, the family disappeared, leaving many people to believe they moved away. I now have a firm conviction that this isn't true. I believe someone walked into their farmhouse in the country and killed the whole family. This murderer is still free and must pay for the crime.

It is my understanding that a young man by the name of Marshall Wallberry loved the eldest daughter, but her father refused to let them marry. Where the young man is today, no one knows. He had two friends, Larry Strandell and Keith Hanselford, who seem to have disappeared as well.

I believe the father, Allen Williams, was not well. He was said to be slightly out of his mind, and that he may even have killed them all, including the boyfriend, and skipped town.

Apparently there was talk about the young couple getting married and running away to the west. Most people believe this is what happened, and that the whole Williams family went with them.

That was before I discovered the graves.

The house where this happened is all boarded up and hasn't been inhabited since. I believe a terrible slaughter took place in that home, and now that I've found the graves I am very puzzled about who boarded up the house-and who buried the bodies in the cemetery.

I discovered that each grave is marked by branches from nearby trees made in the form of crosses. Each cross has an etching that may once have included names or dates. They're weather-beaten and unrecognizable now. If the killer is the one who buried them, I wonder, why go to that trouble?

The house is still there, neglected, long forgotten, and waiting to deteriorate. It sits at the front of many acres of land with a huge barn, sheds, and chicken coops partially fallen down.

The St. Catharines police did investigate when a relative called them to say something was wrong out there. They found the house boarded up, and then they investigated the school to verify that the family had moved. The mother had picked up the children's records and report cards, along with transfers for another school out west. That seemed to satisfy the police.

If you think I'm just some screwball writing a letter, ask your parents about your cousins and what they think happened to them. Scandal sometimes rears its ugly head and people wipe away the evidence, all in the name of family.

If you're still in doubt, go to the cemetery I mentioned. It's just a stone's throw from Dunnville and Welland. You just get off the highway at Grimsby. You can't miss the place. Once you've found the cemetery, go right over a raised mound in the ground and walk to the back near an old fence at the property line. There's a creek several yards beyond this.

Then turn west and walk several feet. There you'll find the shallow graves, marked only by stick crosses and little stones. Don't mistake the sticks for fallen branches.

This is a story that needs to be told. A killer has gone free far too long and needs to be apprehended. Now it's up to you as a reporter to write this story and find out the truth.

She went through the letter's details, feeling as though she were back at school trying to solve a math problem. Supposedly there were seven graves, seven family members, and three young men involved in the story—Marshall Wallberry, Larry Strandell, and Keith Hanselford.

Was one of those men the killer? If so, what had happened to the other two? Did the seven graves belong to the seven members of the Williams family? What a dilemma. It didn't make sense for the boyfriend to kill the girl he loved.

There were just too many questions that didn't have answers.

She was hooked. But could she get James interested? The worst he could do was say no. And if James didn't want her to pursue the story, maybe she could use her holiday time to investigate.

There was a story here, she just knew it.

She left her cubicle and walked to James's office. Hopefully he would see how great the story was. Maybe he would even be the one to suggest that she look into it.

James Creamier was a tall, well-built man. One could even say he was handsome in his old age. Well, not that old. He had a lopsided smile that must have been very sexy when he was young. He still sported a good head of hair, though it was slightly greying at the temples. His very arresting eyes seemed to hold valuable knowledge.

There was no doubt in anyone's mind that he knew the news business inside and out. He was smart and tough with his employees, always expecting the best—and they gave all they had to him. The newspaper was in competition with several others in the towns and cities nearby, so they had to be on the ball.

Alex passed several offices and open areas where people worked. When she arrived at James's open door, she stopped and rapped lightly against the wood.

James looked up from behind his desk.

"May I have a few minutes of your time, James?" she asked. People who didn't know him as well as Alex did called him Mr. Creamier. When his wife came in, she called him Jimmy. That always sounded so strange to Alex. He was definitely not a Jimmy to her.

"Come in, Alex. I'm always glad to see you. What's up?"

She sat in the chair near his desk. "I received a letter addressed to me yesterday and I've been trying to decide if it's something I should look into it."

She handed him the letter, still in the envelope.

He read it not once but three times, her eyes never leaving his face.

James looked down at the letter in his hand, taking note of her name and the date. He actually read it three times. A puzzled frown slid across his face.

"It's interesting, I will say," he began. "So you think there might be a story in this? The handwriting looks exaggerated to me, never mind the content. I think it's just a guy who saw something in the cemetery, heard some old tales in the neighborhood hangout, and let his imagination run away with him. Plus, it's in some forsaken village out in the country…" He paused. "Alex, I think you can throw this letter in the garbage. If the police didn't think anything was wrong, the family probably did just move away. The writer is a crackpot."

Alex knew that he had a way of testing his reporters to make sure they saw a story through to the end if they took it on. For James, making reporters almost beg for it was the only way to go. Then when he agreed, they did an amazing job. Alex was one of his best; still, his way was the best way.

She gave him an unhappy look, but he ignored it. She couldn't ever remember being more sure of a story. Why did it suddenly seem like pulling teeth to get through to him? This certainly wasn't the first time he had turned her down, never mind that she was usually right. She would have to think of another way to get him on her side.

"Here's what I'll do," James finally said, relenting. "Leave the letter with me and let me think about it. By the way, good job on that last story you covered."

"Thanks." She knew she was pushing it a little. "I have a feeling about this letter, James." The puppy dog eyes and turned-down lip sometimes worked on him. "I looked into those three names and they all seem to have disappeared about fifteen years ago. That alone is weird."

"Sure. I admit you have a nose for news, but you can't go out there by yourself. This may be some freak interested in getting you alone in some forsaken cemetery. It could be he just likes pretty girls." James leaned back in his office chair. "Alex, you're a lovely young woman. Even an old duffer like me can see that. You know as well as I do what kind of world we live in today. So let me know if you get another letter."

He reached for a piece of paper sitting on his desk.

"Here's something you can look into that just came in," he

said. "Some guy was just arrested for killing his parents in Toronto. See if you can get an interview with his lawyer. I believe this could make a good story."

"Okay." She let out a huge sigh.

Her disappointment wasn't lost on him. When he saw that Alex's dejected expression hadn't gone away, he almost wanted to smile. "I know that look on your face. Give me your argument for going after the murdered family story."

Her whole body perked up with new excitement. "First, a killer has gotten away with murder—not one, but seven. We need to find him. The oldest daughter may be involved, and those three guys disappeared at the same time. That's not to mention the connection to my own family. I talked to my mother about it and she was very evasive." She cast a glance at him, her eyes begging him. "I need to know the truth."

"I see you're not going to say no to this one easily," he said slowly. "Okay, if you insist on following this, you have my blessing. But look, I want you to be safe. How about taking one of our photographers? Decide who you're taking with you and let me know. And we'll cover your expenses as usual."

Alex smiled at him. "Thanks."

She knew that James had a soft spot for her. After all, he had only sons. He had introduced her to two of them, but she hadn't been interested in either. The feeling had been mutual.

"You know, Alex, I've made some friends who can be very useful in this business," James said after giving it some more thought. He was pleased to see her spirits lift. "I'll call someone who can open the cops' doors for you in St. Catharines and Welland. That's probably the best place to start."

She left his office and began walking back to her cubicle. The more she thought about it, the more excited she got. She refused to believe the letter had been sent by just another weirdo.

She sat down in the comfy chair at her desk, feeling like she had accomplished a lot. Sometimes she felt God leading her to expose something that was wrong and make it right, although she never said this out loud. It had happened several times and had always turned out for the better. She had a nose for news, just as James had said, and loved the excitement of her job. She knew how to look after herself, and there would be little danger if she was careful. She even had a permit to carry a small gun she'd bought.

Now to find someone who would be interested enough to go with her. That may not be easy either. She'd have to sell them on the story too.

"Lord," she said softly, "I need your help again."

"Excuse me," a voice said. Alex turned to find Virginia, her best friend, leaning against the cubicle wall. "You almost looked like you were sleeping. Is something wrong?"

"No, sorry. I was lost in thought. Don't tell me you have nothing to do, Ginny."

"Well, not exactly," Ginny said. "I turned in my stuff on James's desk a couple of hours ago. Now I'm a bit bored and looking for something to do. Something that won't add more stress to my life! I wonder, could you get the afternoon off? I'm having trouble letting the past few months go. I'm sure other people who get divorced have their what-if moments too. I don't think anyone gets over a divorce easily."

Alex felt so sorry for her friend. Ginny's husband had turned out to be a loser. Why some men changed after they tied the knot, she didn't know.

"I'm sorry, I can't," Alex said. "I have a story. Well, sort of a story. I'm about to start investigating something in the Niagara area." She suddenly looked up at her friend, an idea coming to her. "Wait a minute! Why don't you come with me? It would be a great way to take your mind of everything."

"Really?" Ginny's initial excitement gave way to puzzlement. "What kind of story? What about James?"

"He wants me to take a photographer, and that could be you. Wouldn't it be great if he let us do the story together?"

"What kind of story?" Ginny sounded cautious. "The stories you work usually have to do with murder, or worse. I love working on the women's pages. I just finished up covering that huge fashion show at the Exhibition. The clothes were amazing. Apparently bright orange is the thing this summer. I saw the most marvelous orange jumpsuit that would look fabulous on you."

Alex had to smile. After all, Ginny always dressed so smart. Her short copper-red hair was unique with her side bangs. Her eyes had a light greenish sparkle, and her full sexy lips only enhanced her pretty face. She was five-six to Alex's five-eleven; together they were like Mutt and Jeff.

"Ginny, this would be perfect. You said you were bored and I'll need someone to take pictures. You might even find it more exciting than shopping." Alex proceeded to tell her friend about the letter, although she left out some details. She didn't want to scare Ginny off.

"I'm not sure I want that kind of excitement," Ginny said when Alex finished. "Covering that kind of crime could get me killed."

Alex flashed her a smile. "Nonsense. I have never been killed."

"No, but it was close a couple of times. I don't want to get in any shootouts."

"I can guarantee you there won't be any shootouts. Plus, I'm going to take Spider. He'll look after both of us. Come on, live on the dangerous side of life."

Of course, Alex hoped they wouldn't run into the killer. She doubted they'd have to worry about it after all this time. And even if they did find him, his defenses would be down.

She also didn't want to say that she believed the Lord would look after them. Ginny wouldn't want to hear it, and Alex didn't believe that if you deliberately walked out in front of a moving car, God would somehow save you. Every decision came with consequences.

"Alex, I've heard it said that sometimes these weirdos who write letters have nothing better to do than sit around and make up stories," Ginny said. "Maybe he's just looking for recognition."

"I've thought of that," Alex said. "At this point, it could go either way. But the idea of bodies buried in shallow graves? That certainly drew my interest. I want to see for myself." She could still see the doubt in Ginny's eyes. "This could be so interesting, Ginny. I can't ignore it. If the letter is true, I need to find the girl and find out what happened to the three guys. The killer has never been caught. Who knows? Maybe they're dead. Or maybe the killer is dead. His tombstone might read, 'Hell is my home.'"

"Oh, that's an awful thing to say. If he killed all those people, what would stop him from killing us too?"

"Well, first of all, we're going to surprise him. And we're going to get the police involved. They'll make sure we're all right."

Ginny seemed to want to do this and doubt it all at the same time.

Why not? Ginny thought. *Maybe it's time to take some chances. Yes, I can do this. Alex is so adventurous.*

"Okay!" Ginny finally decided. "When do you want to do this?"

"Soon. And don't you have holiday time coming up? So do I. After we finish the story, we can take a couple of weeks together. Even if this doesn't pan out, we'll go and enjoy the Niagara area and eat ourselves through their orchards. Remember all those amazing wholesale shops across the border? Think of all the buys we can get there."

Ginny's eyes came alive with excitement. "Oh, you have me hooked. And we'll have to make a reservation at a nice hotel to stay overnight. The newspaper will cover our expenses, right?"

"Yes, they will. I just have to see James and let him know I'm taking you. Stay here and I'll go see if it's all right."

Alex walked back towards James's office. The door was still open, meaning anyone was welcome to go inside. She walked in and smiled at him.

"James, I have a photographer. You know Virginia Adams, from the women's section of the paper? She's one of my best friends and she's agreed to go with me. Is that all right with you?

James nodded. "Yes. She needs the break. It'll be just what the doctor ordered. It might be good experience for her too. Now, I'm counting on you to use your head, Alex. Pick up some vouchers from the office and keep in touch every day. I mean it, Alex. Every day. If you miss a day, I'll order you back, understand?"

"I will. I promise."

Alex left the office feeling excited. She couldn't wait to tell Ginny as she made her way back to her cubicle to make plans. She had to figure out where they would start.

Ginny was there waiting for her.

"Okay, Ginny, we have the okay. On your way back to your desk, can you pick up the vouchers for us? And you'll need your camera equipment and some clothes for a couple of weeks."

"Okay." Ginny felt a bit nervous, but she was committed now. Her anxiety was trying to spoil the adventure for her.

Alex reminded herself that if this didn't pan out, it would still make for a great paid holiday with her best friend. She could hardly wait to get started.

CHAPTER THREE

A TRIP PLANNED

Alex spent the next hour finishing up work that needed to be completed. She then had to make some sort of plan for the next day. She would start wherever she could get the most assistance from the local police. Hopefully they wouldn't all ignore her and think she was as crazy as the letter writer.

She tried calling several police stations in the area, and they were willing to help but didn't have many resources to spare. Her sad story seemed to be getting her nowhere.

She had just one more call to make: the police in St. Catharines. The phone rang and rang, and she wondered if anyone was there. Maybe word had gotten out about her and they were deliberately ignoring the call. She hoped they weren't giving her the runaround. If they found the killer, it would be a feather in their cap too.

"St. Catharines Police Department," a voice finally answered.

Once again she explained who she was and asked to speak to the chief. Within a minute, she finally heard a not-too-friendly voice identify himself.

"Good afternoon. This is Chief Lorne Merritt. May I help you?"

"Chief, this is Alex Rutherford, a reporter from Oakville News, just south of Toronto." She wanted to sound important. "I received a strange letter in the mail a couple of days ago and it tells an interesting story from your neck of the woods." She explained what it said. "The writer of the letter wants me to think you have a killer in your area of the country that has never been found. I want to investigate it, and I believe it's time we caught him and justice was served."

She hoped that phrasing it this way would catch his interest.

"You can forget that," he said brusquely. "There are a lot of nuts out there, and they're always writing letters. We get them too. And like everyone else, we could use more men and time. I'm sorry."

"But what if this is real?" she asked. "You have a killer on your doorstep. Perhaps you could spare me a man for a week or so. It would mean going back to your cold cases, and you might be able to solve a case. You may not even remember fifteen years back."

"We have the same killings and weird happenings as all places. You know, a father or mother snatches the kids and runs, teens run away, people head for the border. It's probably just some nut with a screw loose." He paused. "Who did you say you were?"

She sighed, hoping he didn't hear it. "Alex Rutherford, from Oakville News. I know what you mean. I get letters all the time and most of them are thrown out, but this one is different. It caught my interest."

"Sorry. I can't help you, Alex. Nevertheless, let me know if you find anything." He hesitated, and his voice got friendlier. "And if you're in my neighborhood, drop in and say hello."

"I'll let you know, and thanks."

Alex hung up and reclined in her chair. *Well, so much for you, Chief Merritt. I'll catch the guy and see what you think then.*

Again, an audible breath escaped her throat.

All these calls had taken a lot out of her. She really couldn't blame the police for being skeptical. He wasn't the friendliest person she had ever talked too. Maybe he was just having a bad day.

She tried to relax, thinking what to do next. She refused to be discouraged. She had been praying about the letter ever since receiving it. She had often found God's answer to be so clear that it left no doubt in her mind as to what she should do. God had many tactful ways of answering prayers.

The rest of the week passed quickly. James had given her the whole following week to look into the letter, so she packed a bag with a variety of clothing options and made a reservation at a bed-and-breakfast in St. Catharines, halfway between the cemetery and the falls. Hopefully they would find the killer and deserve a great vacation. Either way, she would be prepared.

* * *

On Friday morning, her alarm went off exactly at 5:30. She quickly got out of bed and showered.

She often referred to the Bible while working on a story, and today she remembered a passage from the book of Proverbs:

> *For the Lord gives wisdom; from His mouth come knowledge and understanding… When wisdom enters your heart, and knowledge is pleasant to your soul, discretion will preserve you; understanding will keep you…* [2]

This book had lent her help so many times when she needed answers.

She made sure Spider had a good breakfast and a run in the back yard. It was funny; Spider seemed to recognize her anxiety and was almost as excited as she got ready to leave. She fastened him into the Suburban's backseat harness, right behind her. Alex had explained to him that Ginny was coming, too, so he couldn't sit in the front.

---

[2] Proverbs 2:6, 10–11.

As they drove, the early morning breeze blew through the open window. Spider stuck his head out, as happy as any dog could be. He loved car rides more than anything.

Just as she parked in one of the two spots that belonged to Ginny in her friend's underground parking, the elevator doors opened and Ginny stepped out with her luggage. Her bags were all piled on top of each other, the larger one on the bottom with wheels. Alex smiled when she saw the luggage, thankful for her heavy-duty vehicle.

Alex literally sprang from the vehicle. "Get in. I'll put your luggage in the trunk."

The truth was, Alex didn't want Ginny to see what was back there.

"What? I can help surely."

Alex shook her head. "No. That's fine, just hop in. Spider is in the back seat."

"I know I've brought too much luggage."

"No, honest. Just get in the vehicle."

"You're not telling me something. I know you, Alexandria. What are you up to?"

"Nothing. All right. Help me then." Alex hadn't wanted her to notice the shovels, rubber boots, and the rake, among other things. Nonetheless, she opened the trunk.

"There's not much room back here for luggage." Ginny unfastened the strap holding the bags together and handed them to Alex one by one. The larger of the two finally went in, with some squeezing. "You only have one bag? And don't think I won't question why you have a rake and shovels in there too."

"It's rather a long story and I'll explain on the way," Alex said. "We really need to get started." She was just glad Ginny hadn't noticed the boots.

"I'll put the camera equipment on the floor in the back seat," Ginny said. "That way, it'll be easy to get if I need it in a hurry."

As Ginny deposited the camera equipment on the floor, she noticed Alex's tools of the trade—a laptop, an old tape recorder, lots of pads of paper, and a cellphone.

Ginny talked to Spider and rubbed his ears.

"Oh yeah, another thing," Ginny said as she climbed into the passenger seat. "I need a coffee before we get too far. I'm not the digging type, either. You must know that. Alex, if things get gory, I'm going to have trouble getting good pictures. You know how sensitive my stomach is. I do fashion, remember?"

"Don't worry. You won't be digging and it isn't likely to be bloody. After fifteen years, it'll just be bones." Alex couldn't help the heels on Ginny's shoes.

"Just bones." Ginny shook her head back and forth. "I just never thought I'd be digging up bodies—or bones—in a cemetery."

"We aren't going to dig them up, just check them out."

"You know, Alex. When I suggested we go on holiday last month, I was thinking overseas. Like France or somewhere exciting."

"You asked for excitement, didn't you?" Alex remarked. "Well, just maybe you'll get it. Maybe that Prince Charming you're looking for is waiting for you in some nice little town in Niagara."

"I will only accept them dead in a cemetery. I'm off men, Alex…" She trailed off, turning to fix Alex with a steady gaze. "What if there really is a killer and we find the bodies? What will you do then?"

"Cross that bridge when we come to it."

"Don't forget I could use a coffee."

"I have that covered." Alex put the key in the slot, and the Suburban purred like a kitten. They made their way to Main Street. Since it was early, they were slightly ahead of the traffic. Once they started out, however, it was heavy both ways, to Toronto and to Hamilton.

Alex loved the early morning. She rolled her window halfway down to enjoy the warm fresh air. "Ginny, if that breeze is too much I can put on the air."

"No, it's perfect, and Spider looks like he enjoys having his window partly down."

The rush hour traffic got even heavier as they continued along. "I detest those drivers who think they're the only ones on the road," Alex said. "Not to mention the ones who want to push me to go faster. Even then, I'm usually a little over the limit as it is."

"It's too bad we're Christians," Ginny said, gesturing to a passing car, "or you could give that guy the finger."

"Yeah right." Alex laughed. "Never mind. Just smile and say, 'Thank you.' That will work just as well!"

They cruised down the main highway that would take them on to Burlington and the great tall bridge over Lake Ontario. Once they were over that, traffic wouldn't be so bad until they reached Stoney Creek.

"If you look on the floor by your feet, there's a tote bag with a thermos of hot coffee and two mugs," Alex said.

"Oh, that's great," Ginny said. It wasn't Tim's, but it was hot. "You always think of everything."

Within a few minutes, they were both sipping coffee. The radio playing music, they were both looking forward to the trip.

Once Alex was heading west, she felt like they were really on their way. The scenery was amazing as they got out of town and its neighbors. They caught glimpses of Lake Ontario here and there in its glorious blues and greens. The sun sparkled like a billion diamonds atop the water.

An hour and forty-five minutes later, they drove into Burlington. Alex turned to pass under the high bridge. This would be a slower route, but there would be more places to stop and she was ready to stretch her legs. Spider needed the stop too. She was thankful they had been making good time.

"Okay, Spider, time for a break and a snack," Alex said. "Ginny, I hope you're ready for a snack too."

"I'll take Spider for a walk under the bridge while you get us a snack," Ginny said. She was glad that Alex had brought the dog. Two women alone weren't always safe, and Spider was better than any man.

They parked and locked the vehicle. Ginny took the dog for a walk and the stop he needed.

Alex soon returned with banana muffins and more coffee. They found a picnic table to sit at and ate while Spider devoured a small portion of food Alex had brought along. They were about to go when a man walked up to them.

"Will he bite?" he asked, smiling at them.

"That all depends on the person who approaches him," Alex said. "He likes most people, but he seems to know the bad ones." Right then, a little rumble came formed in his throat. "Spider is very protective of us."

"What kind of breed is he?" the man asked.

"He's a cross between Collie and a Spaniel."

"He is a gorgeous dog. And he has amazing color. I can see where he got his name from." When he looked right at the dog, Spider growled softly, sounding scary. Spider was putting on a good show for him. "I admit he doesn't look that friendly. But then, I suppose that's a good thing for two beautiful ladies traveling alone these days."

Alex didn't like him and didn't like his reference to them being alone, and it was obvious Spider didn't either.

"We can both look after ourselves. If you'll excuse us, we're on a schedule." Alex stood up. The picnic bench was hard anyway.

"Well, have a nice day."

"You too."

Once they were on their way, both women felt better. Soon they were back on the highway in the flow of cars, heading south. They passed several new hotels going up. She was astonished at the changes going on since the last time she had driven here.

Alex's mind wandered to their destination, and to wondering what lay ahead.

Finally, they took an exit off the Queen Elizabeth Highway and came to the town of Winona on the way to Smithville. Next, she took a jog along another small highway, heading toward Canborough. The road was well paved and fairly busy.

They passed some lovely villages. The drive was beautiful and the scenery lush, with farms dotting the countryside. They passed fields of grapevines, and several large wineries. Other fields were ripe with cherry trees and pick-your-own strawberries patches. The orchards of peach trees weren't ready for harvest yet.

When they saw a sign announcing Canborough a few miles ahead, Alex pulled back a bit on the speed and suddenly wasn't so sure she wanted to do this after all.

Ginny felt the vehicle slow down.

"You know, we don't have to do this," Ginny said. "But I know you, Alex. You'll never be satisfied until you prove the letter was fake and all this anxiety was for nothing."

Alex knew her friend was right. "To be honest, I don't know what I want to find. Part of me wants it to be real and wants the story, no matter how awful it is. Another part of me wants it all to be nothing so we can go on and have a nice holiday."

A few minutes later, they arrived in the village of Canborough.

"It looks like we're here, only you've passed the cemetery," Ginny pointed out. "Have you changed your mind?"

"No. I just wanted to see if I felt any ghosts." Alex laughed. She came to a bridge over a small creek. She wondered if it was the same creek that supposedly ran behind the cemetery the letter spoke of. There were a couple of churches, but it was otherwise a small village.

"Ghosts? What are you talking about?"

"My grandmother lived here, and her mother lived on a farm nearby. I had a lot of relatives around here, as I understand it, and they date back to the 1700s. I was born in Dunnville, not far away." Alex stopped the Suburban along the side of the road. "My mother has really been into family history the last few years. She keeps all that stuff in boxes. One day it will be mine, and I plan to put it all into a book for the generations to come."

"My family comes from Nova Scotia," Ginny said. "When I was a kid, we visited here, but I don't remember much about it. My grandparents moved to Quebec for a while and finally ended up in Ottawa, where I was born. When I met Tom, we moved to Toronto. You know the rest."

Alex found herself getting lost in old memories of her grandmother's stories. When she was a kid, her grandmother had loved to go over and over the past. It had always fascinated Alex.

"In the old days, people attended two churches, one in the morning and the other at night," Alex said. "My grandmother had an Aunt Alice, whom she adored, and she always went to church with her at night. Church and the love of God were very important to my grandparents, as they were to all the people around here. The church was the centerpiece of the village. She's gone now, but I'll always remember her." She took a deep breath. "Well, enough nostalgia for now. We have to go into that cemetery."

Alex turned the vehicle around and headed back towards the cemetery they'd passed on their way into town.

CHAPTER FOUR

THE CEMETERY

Alex and Ginny sat parked on the side of the road for several minutes.

"Honestly, Alex, this cemetery is big, and it's still being used by the looks of it. See those flowers on the graves? People must come here. But from what you told me, it sounded like the cemetery would be old and forgotten. Maybe we're in the wrong place?"

"I agree. This isn't what I imagined at all." Alex was once again in doubt about the letter. But she had come all this way. She would check it out, no matter what. "I don't see how the letter can be right, but I followed the directions carefully. This has to be it."

"Maybe somehow you screwed up. Do you have the directions with you?"

"Yes, I do. This is the place." She pointed at the sign out front. "It even has the same name on the plaque. Melick Cemetery."

She handed the instructions to Ginny, who looked at them and then at the sign.

"By the looks of it, we can drive right in," Ginny said. There appeared to be no roadway, but two fairly good tracks that other cars had used. "Alex, if there really is a killer and such a family really existed, they must have been from around here to know about this cemetery. Oh! And if the letter is true, then the guy who wrote it must be from here too. What if he's sitting someplace nearby with a pair of field glasses, just watching us?"

"First of all, he doesn't know for sure that I would investigate it. And I seriously doubt that the killer is the same guy who wrote the letter. Why would he? He doesn't want to get caught and go to jail for the rest of his life either. Let's get this over with."

Alex started the vehicle again and slowly made her way into the cemetery. They could both hear overgrown weeds brushing against the side of the vehicle, burnt dry by the sun. Most of the tombstones glistened in the sunlight. In spite of it being a cemetery, there was something peaceful about the place. If one ignored the tombstones, it could be a park.

"We can be thankful the ground is hard and dry, or we might get stuck in here," Ginny said. "I don't suppose we have to worry about snakes and stuff when it's so dry either. You probably thought of that, never mind the scratches on your vehicle."

"Yes, I did. And I actually brought rubber boots along, just in case we needed them."

"Rubber boots. Oh great."

They had driven well into the cemetery when Alex stopped again. "It seems to me we're a good halfway in, if not a bit more. This seems as good a spot as any to park."

Alex parked the vehicle, but they didn't get out. Spider lolled his head out the window, looking about. It just seemed so quiet, even in the sunlight.

"From what the letter said, the graves aren't easily seen," Alex said. "The place is over a rise in the earth, towards the back. The letter talks about the land dropping down to a small creek."

"Let's look around and get the lay of the land," Ginny said. "You're sure you want to do this? I already have a creepy feeling. Do you think these dead people know we're here?"

"If they did, they wouldn't mind. We're here to do something good, and besides, where in the Bible would you find something like that? Absent from the body, present with the Lord."

"Yeah. But someday the bodies are supposed to come out of the graves."

"Not today. And even if it were, we would already be in the clouds with Jesus by then."

"What about all the evil ones still hanging around the earth?" Ginny asked. "Where are they?"

"Not here, I can assure you."

They left the vehicle and Alex studied the ground. The sun had really parched the ground here.

"Hold on a minute, Alex. My shoes aren't meant for this kind of walking. I'll take a pair of the boots." It took a few minutes to get them on. She hopped about for a while, getting used to the feel of them.

They started to walk, examining the tombstones as they went, reading dates and names. Spider led the way, sniffing and doing what dogs do.

After they had walked some distance, Alex hated to admit that she couldn't see anything like what the letter had described. But it wasn't a total waste of time. She found graves that belonged to some of her ancestors. She would have to ask her mother for more information on them.

They came to a stop on a knoll, looking ahead as the earth sloped down. There was nothing to see except old whitewashed stones that looked ancient. Some had toppled over, long forgotten by the world. It was easy to see that this part of the cemetery hadn't been used for years, perhaps going back to the early 1700s.

"Have you had enough?" asked Ginny. She knew by now that the letter was a phony.

"I have to go right down to the back of the cemetery to be positive."

"You're sure? The ground is scorched." Ginny looked down the hill. "Well, it does look very overgrown in that direction by the trees."

Alex cast a glance at Spider. "We're going looking for bones, Spider. Not your kind of bones, though."

Alex made a low humming noise and Spider barked as if he completely understood.

As they set out again, Ginny was glad she had changed into boots. She kept thinking about what might be living in the long grass and weeds the sun hadn't burned off. Not to mention the snakes in the forgotten earth beneath her feet. She constantly looked where she stepped.

They both stopped at the howl of a wolf afar off. Sounds played a huge part in firing Ginny's imagination. Everything from the wind rustling a tree branch or the scurry of some little unseen creature in their path made her stop in her tracks.

Finally they made it to the bottom. While neither of them believed in ghosts, they had an eerie feeling while standing in the tall grass, especially since they couldn't see the vehicle anymore.

"I'm keeping my eye on Spider," Ginny said. "If I suddenly see the hair on his back stand up straight, I'm out of here."

Alex smiled at her friend, but she felt disappointed. This seemed to have turned into a wild goose chase. For the life of her, she couldn't believe the whole letter had been a lie.

"There doesn't look to be anyone buried back here," Alex said at last. "I hate to say it, but I'm disappointed."

"Sorry. To be honest, I'm not," Ginny said. "Did you happen to notice that we can't see the front of the cemetery from here? It didn't look like so much of a hill at first, but it does now."

Spider seemed to like it. Alex let out his leash so he could run around a bit more. The grass here was in a shaded area that probably got little sunlight.

"Did it ever occur to you that snakes might live in this kind of long grass?" Ginny asked.

Alex dared not look down or Ginny would hightail it back to the Suburban. Alex put her hand on an old, broken-down fence that stood between the cemetery and the bush beyond. From here, she could see a creek just a few feet away. Beyond that was nothing but more wilderness and forest. It looked very much like the letter had described.

"We have to look a bit more," Alex said. "Let's walk on, keeping several feet away from the fence. We need to look for anything that might look like a shallow grave. We can't give up now."

Alex failed to noticed Ginny's mournful glance in her direction. "You must be kidding. How would I know what a shallow grave looks like?"

"It would be about six feet by four feet, more or less, and the ground will be sunken."

They both started to walk again, Ginny hoping she wouldn't find such a thing. She didn't want to be a poor sport, so she walked very slowly, almost afraid to take each step. She just wanted to get on with their holiday.

Alex walked slowly too, watching for anything that looked like a grave. Every once in a while, she stopped and examined the earth about her before deciding it was nothing but uneven ground.

They have to be here, she kept thinking. The awful thing was, she wanted them to be here. And that made her feel even worse. If they were out west, at least they weren't dead.

After about twenty minutes, when Alex was about to give up, she stopped in her tracks. Her foot had caught on a root, and then she noticed a small slab of stone. It could have been a grave marker, she supposed, although there was no headstone. It was just her imagination.

"The letter said there are stick-like crosses," Alex said, excitement creeping up on her again. "Tell me if you see anything like that."

"What exactly is a stick-like cross?"

"I presume crosses made from tree branches. Like markers, for the graves."

Ginny bent over to study the ground, moving the earth as best she could. Suddenly, a dog's nose appeared right beside her own.

"Get back, Spider." Ginny pushed him away so she could have a better view. Then she noticed something rather peculiar. Her finger caught on a tree branch that seemed to sink a fair way into the ground. She grasped it and pulled. Once it was in her hand she discovered there was a second branch, fastened with wild grass reeds to form a cross. She lifted it to her face to get a better look at it. The longer piece was about fourteen or sixteen inches long, and the shorter one was about five inches.

"Ginny, look at this!" Alex called, holding two branches in her hand. Then she noticed that Ginny had a similar pair of branches in her own hands.

"Before you get all excited," Ginny said, "if I remember my history, people used wooden crosses to mark graves before the use of cement or stone. Although I believe they were made with sturdier wood, not branches."

Alex was sure these weren't errant tree branches. They were crosses, constructed with care.

"Notice the work in the binding," Alex said. "Nature certainly didn't do this."

Ginny couldn't help but agree.

"See how many more we can find." Alex said.

They walked around carefully, their eyes focused on the ground. Sure enough, almost in a row they discovered what appeared to be seven graves with crosses—or what was left of them.

"The ground is sunken, like you said, but that's normal if a grave isn't looked after," Ginny said. "These people were probably buried here in the 1700s."

"Maybe. Or maybe not. If these graves were old, they probably would have been marked with better crosses, not branches. See the broken branches on the ground? I can imagine someone sitting on the ground and whittling these with a jackknife, taking his time as he buried each body."

A creepy feeling danced up and down Ginny's spine. "Do you know how gross that sounds?"

Ginny leaned down and picked up another of the crosses—no easy feat, since it had been planted deep in hard soil. As she inspected it, she noticed something strange.

"Alex, this is odd. It looks like an etching in the wood. Could it be a date?" It looked like it had been etched, but the inscription had been worn away with time. "Oh Alex, this is what you are looking for! If you look where you're standing, the ground is solid. But if you stand back, you can see the imprint of each grave."

Alex stepped back and counted. From where she was standing, there were absolutely seven graves. It was like a miracle they had found them. Her face lit up with excitement.

A great moan escaped Ginny's mouth as she shook her head. "What are we going to do?"

Alex wanted to shout for joy. The letter was real!

Ginny moaned again. She knew exactly what her friend intended to do—dig up the graves. "Alex, you can't disturb these graves. It's against the law! We could be arrested."

"Okay, so we'll just trample down the dead grass and weeds to make sure these are actually sunken graves."

"Yeah right. You want me to step on the bodies?"

"They'll just be old bones—and if they were that close to the surface, animals would have gotten them by now. Besides, don't you think these victims, whoever they were, would want some sort of justice for their deaths?"

"I suppose so, but I'm not sure they would want to be trampled on." When Ginny looked at the ground, she could almost imagine a bony hand reaching up from the earth and grabbing the ankle of her boot in protest.

"You know something?" Alex said. "In this case, I reason it's more important to break the law than keep it."

Ginny had never heard her say anything like that before. "I don't think you should dig up a grave without the family's consent."

"Right, only there's no family we know of, let alone a name or a proper burial. It's just a place where some maniac buried his victims."

"Oh Alex, sometimes I think your imagination overtakes your common sense. Maybe this was normal a hundred years ago. We don't know for sure that these people were killed." Ginny paused to think about it some more. "But maybe we do need to dig up a body, to check it before saying anything to anyone." She let out another moan. "I'm starting to sound like you."

Alex was well aware of how excited her friend had become. That was a good thing. "We need the shovels," she said. "Let's see if we can drive the Suburban closer."

"Just don't get us stuck in here."

"I won't."

Spider bounded ahead, having a good run as he led them back up the hill.

CHAPTER FIVE

AN INTERESTING FIND

Neither Alex nor Ginny could believe they had found the graves, but now they had to make a huge decision about what to do next.

"Technically, we won't know if they're graves until we dig them up," Alex said.

"I knew you were going to say that," Ginny said. "So what are we looking for? A skull or something like that? Is your stomach prepared?" Her hand rested for a second on her stomach. "Believe it or not, you have me curious. I hate to admit, but I couldn't leave now without knowing for sure."

They both stood staring at the ground by their feet. They stood just to the side; it seemed disrespectful to stand right on it.

"If we find bones, I'll call the St. Catharines police chief. It might be fun to hear what he has to say now, after turning me down. Then he can get his officers to do the rest."

They walked back to the vehicle. Spider climbed in, thinking they were going home.

"Sorry, Spider," Alex said. "We're not leaving yet. The adventure is just beginning."

They soon were back at the bottom of the hill, shovels, gloves, and a rake in hand. Alex had also brought some plastic gloves from the trunk.

Alex placed her foot on the edge of the shovel blade and pushed it into the hard soil at the top of one grave. She dug very carefully, finding the soil to be a mix of sand and clay. She didn't want to dig too deep, so as not to destroy anything she might find.

Shovel by shovel, the dirt began to pile up. When Alex was satisfied that she had gone deep enough, she used a rake to slowly scrape the dirt aside. She came to what looked like a piece of clear plastic material and stopped. She bent down, dropping the rake.

Ginny took a great gulp of air. *What a relief,* she thought. *It's just garbage.*

"Ginny, I need you to take the rake and go real slow as I carefully pull on this plastic. I don't want to disturb whatever's in there. I just need to see inside."

"Are you sure? What if it's just garbage? Imagine the smell."

"Just go slowly. Rake right to the edge so I can get a hold of it."

"Okay." She did as Alex said, not sure if she really wanted to. She felt a combination of fear and apprehension.

Even Spider got in on the act. He looked over Alex's shoulder and she had to push him back. He was more interested in the smell than what was really going on.

"Oh Alex, that shouldn't be there," Ginny said when she caught a glimpse of what they were unearthed. It looked like bone.

With her hands in outdoor gloves, Alex felt something hard. There was definitely something there. She took the spoke of the other rake and used it to rip the edge of the plastic some more. As she pulled on the plastic, looking closer, she found herself staring at a skull. For one second, she didn't know what to do. The air seem to thicken and close, making it impossible to breath. Her heart beat faster with emotion.

That skull had at one time belonged to a person made of flesh and blood. Alex's body went from hot to cold several times. She wanted to fill the grave back in, but instead she just squatted there, staring at it. A few strands of hair still clung to the skull, above the gaping black holes where eyes should have been.

"The rest of the bones must be in the plastic," Ginny said. To her surprise, she bent down to examine the skull more closely. It was quite clean and weird to touch with her gloved hand. Suddenly aware of what she was doing, she tried to put the plastic back around the shoulder bones and skull. It wouldn't go back exactly as it had been.

"I think we need to cover it back up for the time being," Alex said, surprised at Ginny's sudden bravery. "Don't let Spider dig it back up again."

It took them a few minutes to put the earth back. Then Alex moved on to the grave right beside it.

"Oh no, Alex. One is enough."

"I have to know if there's more, to prove what the letter said. Come on, it's not so bad."

"Alex, it's awful. I'll have nightmares for weeks to come."

"You'll be fine. Go take Spider for a walk and I'll handle this."

"And leave you here? No way. Carry on and get it over with."

Alex smiled at her, then went through the same routine. It took longer the second time, but resulted in the same discovery. The letter had been true; here she stood in the middle of a killer's burial ground.

I can't for the life of me imagining a man killing a whole family, Alex thought.

"What's the matter?" Ginny called. She hadn't moved one step.

"The person who wrote that letter was telling the truth. There are several stones in a row here, almost like markers. Have you any idea what this means?"

"I'm not sure I want to know."

"Ginny, go back to the Suburban and get your camera equipment. I need pictures of all this, every gravesite, including this one I've just dug up. I'm not going to fill this one in. I'm going to leave it for the cops. Come on, this is your chance to shine. Give me perfect pictures from every angle. It's easy to see where they are now that we've trampled down the long grass."

Forgetting everything else, Ginny ran back to the vehicle. In no time, she was back and taking pictures. She bent and twisted to get just the right angles.

"Even after fifteen years, this plastic wrap is in almost perfect condition," Alex mused. "Those environmentalists are right. Plastic must be really bad for our landfills."

Ginny ignored her. "Fine. Now that we have pictures, let's call the cops. Better yet, let's just make a run for it and let someone else discover this mess."

Ginny started to walk away, but Alex followed right behind her.

"No way Jose!" Alex said. She suddenly stopped and looked back. For one second, she couldn't believe her eyes. It was as if the corpses had come alive. They seemed to stand in the flesh, all in a row, one on each grave and looking right at her.

She blinked and they were gone. Had she just seen ghosts from the past? What a strange experience that was. No one would believe such a thing.

"What's the matter?" asked Ginny.

"Nothing. I was thinking it just seemed weird as I stood looking back at all those graves. We don't know what they suffered before they died. Ginny, I'm so glad we came and didn't give up. We're going to get justice for these people. "

"Don't think that way! They may have died quickly. You don't know anything about them."

"No, but I can guarantee you that I will. Their story is going to be told." Alex took her cellphone out of her pocket. It was like a brick and resembled a walky-talky. "I'm going to call Chief Merritt. He's in charge of the cop shop in St. Catharines."

She pressed in his number and put it to her ear and listened for it to ring. She was slightly impatient, waiting for it to be answered.

"Chief Lorne Merritt here," the man answered.

"Chief, it's Alexandria Rutherford. I talked to you yesterday."

"I recognize your voice. You're the reporter from Oakville. Dare I ask when you're coming to my neck of the woods?"

"I'm here," she said with a laugh. "Actually, I'm in that cemetery I told you about."

"Really? I was curious after your call and took a drive out there, but I couldn't find anything like what you told me about. Then again, I wasn't really sure what I was looking for. Are you there now?"

"Yes, I am, and the letter writer was right. There are graves here, enough for a whole family. I removed the earth from the top of a couple of graves, and in both cases I found bones wrapped in plastic. I had to be sure."

"You what?" Merritt said, alarmed. "You're kidding!"

"No, sorry. You're going to need a whole crew out here with shovels and whisks to get the bones out of the ground."

"Okay, Ms. Rutherford, and please don't touch anything else. We'll be about thirty minutes getting there. I'll leave right away."

The phone went dead.

CHAPTER SIX
HERE COME THE COPS

Lorne sat in his office for a minute, trying to recall every word the reporter had said. He shook his head, thinking the whole story was unbelievable. Well, he had no choice now but to look into this. As if they weren't busy enough! He picked up the phone from his desk and called his right-hand man, Phil Hudson.

"Phil here. What can I do for you, Lorne?"

"Phil, I told you about that reporter who phoned me. You won't believe this. She's here, in that country cemetery. She's found the graves…" He paused. "…and she's dug them up, or something like that."

"Dug up what? You've lost me." In his own office, Phil scratched an itch on his forehead, listening but not understanding.

"*Bodies*, I presume. Several, if I what she says is true. I need you put a crew together and meet me out there as soon as possible, with shovels and whatever we'll need to do the job. And we need to get there before she messes up the whole crime scene."

Phil pictured bodies strewn in the open, gathering dust and flies. His face contorted. He really didn't want to see any of this.

"Right away, Lorne."

Why would some reporter do such a thing? Phil asked himself. *Maybe Lorne has misunderstood somehow. Yes, that has to be it.*

Lorne gave him directions to Canborough and then hung up.

Phil put the phone back on the cradle and carried on getting a crew assembled for the job.

He had never heard anything like this before in his whole life. He had seen some dandies, but this beat them all. He got up from his chair, grabbed the keys for his police car, and made his way to the parking lot.

* * *

Ginny watched her friend and cohort in crime put down the phone. What they were doing had to be against the law. She hoped James would bail them out of jail if they got arrested for digging up corpses.

"He didn't believe me the first time, but he will now," Alex said. "I need a little time to boast, Ginny. These guys think women aren't as capable as they are. Never mind. We'll show them."

Ginny glanced at Alex and smiled. Her friend was such a woman-libber. She did make her laugh sometimes.

They stood waiting on the rise in the earth, waiting for the police to come.

It seemed to take them long enough. At last, a police cruiser made its way into the cemetery. The vehicle moved over sunburnt brush and bumped its way through ruts before stopping next to the Suburban.

Two well-built officers got out of the cruiser and walked toward them, strolling down the hill over the dry grass and weeds. Alex couldn't take her eyes off the taller one; his muscles seemed to ripple as he drew nearer.

"Umm, this might be interesting after all," Alex said. "It helps when they're big strong guys. And there's one for each of us."

"Bite your tongue. No thanks," Ginny replied. "They're probably married with a flock of kids."

Alex smiled, remembering that her friend had said she was off men.

Spider started to bark and growl to show he meant business. He moved closer to Alex.

"Quiet, Spider," Alex said. "They're all right."

Ginny was surprised that the dog was so aggressive. He would be a good protector after all.

"Excuse me, ladies," the taller officer said as they approached. "I hope that dog doesn't want me for dinner."

"Spider's just protective of me," Alex said. "That's all."

"I'm Chief Lorne Merritt," he added, introducing himself. He stopped in front of the two women, wondering which one was Alex. He thought they both looked very attractive—and young. Not what he had been expecting. They didn't look the kind to dig up bodies.

"Hi Chief," Alex said. "I'm Alex Rutherford and this is my photographer, Ginny Adams."

He nodded and indicated the second offer. "This is Detective Philip Hudson. It's nice to meet you both."

Phil gave Ginny a flirtatious wink. "Hi, Ginny."

"Ms. Rutherford, you have me curious," Lorne said. "I don't want to admit it, but if you have found the Williams family, I'm glad you came out here. If these are murder victims, then it's about time they were found. So let's go see what you have."

"Do you mind the dog?" Alex asked. "I have him on his leash and he'll stay right at my side."

"That's all right." Lorne wondered if she didn't trust him, so he plastered a smile onto his face. He had no idea what they were in for. He didn't see any graves like the ones she had told him about.

"Chief, before we get to the graves, I'd like you to look at this letter." Alex took the piece of paper from her pocket and handed it to him. She watched him open it and read.

"I'm surprised you didn't just think some nut wrote it," Lorne said when he was done. "If it had been me, I would have ignored it." He handed the letter to Phil to read. "Then again, he probably knew you would look into it. I have to say, it's a good thing you did."

Phil read it a couple of times as well and then looked up. "I have to admit, it would be difficult not to check this out."

"I did quite a lot of thinking before making a decision," Alex said. "Then I had to sell my editor on it."

"Show me where you found these graves," Lorne said. "Please, lead the way."

Lorne wondered at her nerve. He would play along—after all, she had been right in every way so far. As long as she kept out of the way of the crime scene, he wouldn't object to her being here.

Alex held Spider's leash close as they approached the gravesites. "They're along the fence line at the bottom of this hill."

When they arrived, Alex watched as the two officers stood over the graves with shocked expressions. Their eyes were fixed on the skull and the bones sticking out of the plastic. She rather enjoyed their surprise, and even smiled a little.

"I told you, I had to be sure," she said. "I found seven crosses made of sticks, just like the letter said. I believe you need to start looking for this family's killer. I can tell you right now, it won't be easy."

She bent down and handed Lorne one of the crosses so he could see the illegible etching in the wood.

He took the cross from her and stared at it disbelievingly.

"I didn't bring a shovel with me," Lorne said. "We have a crew on the way, though, and they should be here soon. I don't suppose you would lend me your shovel? You know, the one you brought just in case you got stuck out here and needed to get the vehicle out?" He wore a grin on his face.

"It's right over there, in the back of my Suburban. I'll get it for you," Alex said. "You're right. It was just in case we got stuck."

It only took her a few minutes to jog back and get the shovel. He handed the shovel to Phil.

"Where do you want me to dig?" Phil asked. "Where the skull is?"

"I suppose it really doesn't matter. You might as well start there."

"This whole thing is bizarre," Alex said. "That is, unless there's an explanation we know nothing about. Perhaps someone who's lived in the area for years could enlighten us. I suppose the final answer lies with a coroner."

"I don't think the coroner will believe this either," Lorne said. "I also have to find out what legal rights we have here. By the way, I'll let you off the hook for digging up the earth. Truth it, you've been such a help to us."

She wanted to say thanks, but she didn't.

At that moment, several additional police cars arrived. A whole crew from the St. Catharines Police Department got out as Lorne went up to talk to them. He explained the problem and set them to work taking pictures, reminding them how careful they had to be to keep each grave and set of remains separate.

"I'll call the coroner," Lorne told them. "Once he arrives, it's going to take some time to dig up all the bodies properly and collect the evidence. It helps that the bodies are wrapped in plastic."

From what Alex could see, the bones were surprisingly well preserved, although some had been found by critters and creepy crawlers hunting for a snack.

"Alex, I'm puzzled about another matter," Lorne said to her as the rest of the men got to work. "Does this have anything to do with your family, like the letter said?"

"I think that was only there to get my interest."

"Then why not send it to a closer newspaper? Like the ones in Thorold or Welland? Oakville is so far away."

"Maybe so this couldn't be swept under the rug like it was originally," Alex said. "He's trying to expose the killer, and the killer may be nearby. Maybe he's right here in this area."

Lorne sighed. "A big part of me would love to cover this back up and walk away, pretend like I never heard of you. I don't suppose that's a possibility."

She had to smile at him. "You could do that?"

"No, but wouldn't it be nice? I don't know how you work, but I'd like to keep this between us for the time being."

"I'd be delighted, as long as you don't tell your local paper. I want to break this myself." Alex looked up into his eyes. "You know, Chief, we don't have the real story yet, but you have information in your archives that I can't get to. We could work the case together. And when we're done, the story will go my paper. It's up to you, Chief. You're in charge."

"Right!" He grinned at her. "Here you are, spoiling all the townsfolk's gossip. St. Catharines is just like Toronto, only smaller. We have perverts, drunks, junkies, dopers, and even murderers. No different than the big city."

"I suppose you're right."

"Look, to be honest, the cops around here won't like the idea that a killer's been lying low so long. The mayor will probably want it kept quiet until we know more of what's going on. This is, after all, tourist country. I'd like to see what my crew can come up with on the quiet. When we know what's going on, we'll let whoever needs to know what's up. But only then."

"Deal." Alex hesitated. "We must remember that there's another person in this scenario: the letter writer. If we can find him, hopefully he'll be able to lead us to the killer."

Lorne wore a serious expression as he called the coroner, telling him what they were dealing with. Then he called the local judge and asked what he could do about getting all the bodies dug up. The judge told him to do it, since they couldn't identify the victims any other way. Finally, Lorne asked the judge to keep it quiet until they knew for sure what they had found.

Forty-five minutes later, two vans arrived from the city morgue. Lorne filled in the coroner about the discovery. The coroner was shocked beyond words, walking from grave to grave and staring at the partially covered bones. He was so thankful that the officers had kept the remains just as they had found them.

The coroner had never seen anything like this before. They would have to be very careful transporting them. Each bag of bones was a person. They would have to find out who they were and how they had died. This was going to be an interesting challenge.

"Luke, I need you to examine them as quickly as possible," Lorne said to the coroner. "We're expecting they were murdered, maybe even by a serial killer. I'll need you to confirm how they died."

"I can't do anything here," Luke said. "How in the world did you come upon something like this? It's like something you see on the news and never expect to come in contact with. Why, you must have six or seven bodies here."

Lorne told him what had happened so far, although he kept a lot of details secret.

"I need you to keep this from the public until I know exactly what we're looking at," Lorne said. "Anyway, it looks like my men are done taking pictures." He turned back to Alex and Ginny. "I presume you've booked a room for tonight in one of the hotels."

"I have, yes. At a bed-and-breakfast," Alex said. "We'll be fine. But I want to go to the morgue with you when you go. I have to know if it's possible these are the bodies of that family. I can't imagine there being any other answer. I hope the coroner can at least tell us how they died, and their ages. I know it will take time to identify who was who."

"That letter will help us a lot too," Lorne said. "I guess your friend got all the pictures she wanted for you to use later?"

"Yes. And we'll go over them carefully before they're ever printed."

Lorne gave her the address and time to meet him at the hospital the following afternoon.

Alex and Ginny climbed into their vehicle and followed Lorne's police cruiser back towards St. Catharines.

The women were both quiet and deep in thought as they drove. Soon they were in St. Catharines, driving over the Welland Canal Parkway. They followed the cruiser for a few more blocks, then turned right. It wasn't long before they stopped outside a large house.

"It looks nice," Alex said. And it was a good thing, since they were going to be a while investigating this case.

Both tired, they took their travel bags from the trunk, as well as Spider. In no time they were registered and shown to their rooms by a very nice lady. Alex's bedroom was equipped with a large television and stereo. The walls were painted a lovely pale green and yellow. There was even a chaise lounge for reading.

Alex opened the door to the room next door, where Ginny was staying. It was decorated very similarly to hers.

They unpacked and found a small diner nearby to go for dinner. Afterward they retired early, exhausted from the long day.

* * *

The next morning, Alex and Ginny got up early and had a delicious breakfast that the owner had prepared for them. Alex got out her laptop and did some work at her room's small desk while Ginny relaxed with a good book.

"It's time to go," Alex said after a while. "Ginny, I can go alone if you want to rest here. Or you can come with me."

Spider gave Ginny a slight bark, as though to encourage her.

"Are you kidding?" Ginny asked. "I'm coming. You're not getting rid of me that easily."

Alex handed her the map as they headed back out to the Suburban. "Okay, lead me to the hospital."

They had a quick sandwich and a pop at a fast food restaurant. After a few wrong turns, they were on their way.

CHAPTER SEVEN

BACK TO THE CEMETERY

A lex pulled the vehicle into the hospital parking lot. She was sure the others would all be here by now. The morgue was one place she really didn't care to go to. Back in Oakville, they had to go to the one in Toronto, and reporters were seldom let in. She couldn't imagine working in such a place.

"You found us," a man's voice said.

Alex turned to see Lorne and Phil crossing the lot.

"I was just coming out to see if you were waiting for me," Lorne said.

"We just got here. The bed-and-breakfast seems to be a nice place. The owner is very friendly."

"Good. The coroner has all the bones laid out on a few tables his department borrowed from the lab. It's too soon to know much and the coroner isn't sure about the timeline yet. He'll know more in a few days, but so far we can only tell there are seven skulls, and presumably seven bodies. They've been in the ground for many years. He thinks fifteen is a good guess. Come in, and the coroner can explain what he thinks."

The four of them walked into a large cool room. Alex shivered as they approached the coroner, whom she recognized from the cemetery. Lorne had called him Luke.

"I'm sure you must be amazed at what you've found," Luke said to her and Ginny. "I can't give you a time of death yet, but if this is the family you suspect, we should be able to get their birth records without too much trouble."

The women followed Luke to the first table. On it was a skeleton, every bone in place. With some imagination, Alex could picture it as a person without skin. She turned her eyes from the skull.

"The chief tells me he thinks they may have been killed close together, maybe even the same day," Luke continued. "This is the first one you dug up, and he could be the eldest. It's obviously male, but it'll take time to tell much more. You can see that he died of a bullet wound, right in the temple. It appears to me you have more males than females, and as to size or age, at this point I can't help you.

"The females are all more or less the same size, so age will be a problem. In some families, the kids are as big as their parents. We may be able to verify their identities through dental records, and also maybe give you some idea where they were killed. It's impossible at this time to establish that." He paused. "It is murder, though, and I'll do my best to come up with answers as soon as I can. I'm glad I'm not in your shoes now."

Even though he had all these bones, and seen some dreadful murders in his years, he was boggled by it.

"Thanks a lot," Lorne said. "Let me know the minute you find anything." He turned to Alex and Ginny with an expression of genuine care and concern. "Let's go. If your stomach will take food, we should get something to eat. Phil and I are going to lunch at a nice restaurant I know. Can I treat you both?"

Alex nodded. "Sure, I could eat. But I'll pay our way. We're on the newspaper's budget."

She was a very independent woman. He might as well know that now.

They made their way back to the vehicle where Spider waited, hooked up to his leash just outside the Suburban. He was straining against it, sniffing the grass. There was a nice stretch of grass along the side of the parking lot that served Spider's purpose perfectly.

They set off in separate vehicles again, with the men in the lead. This time Ginny drove, frustrated as traffic kept getting between her and the police cruiser.

Mama Rose's was small but homey. They were seated at a table in the corner of the dining room, and it was only ten minutes before they were served salads of their choice, soft homemade rolls, and tall glasses of ice water with lemon on the side.

They ordered the house specialty: spaghetti with vegetables and a large chicken breast cut into strips. It was cooked to perfection and certainly filled their empty stomachs. Lunch was followed by homemade plumb pie and ice cream. They made fruit pies one would never find anywhere else.

They didn't talk once about the case, focusing instead on getting to know each other. Ginny couldn't believe Phil was a Christian. In fact, they had a lot in common. It turned out he had never been married, though he had gotten close two times only to discover the girl wasn't right for him.

After dinner, Alex and Ginny headed back to the bed-and-breakfast. They watched the late news together, glad there was nothing mentioned about the cemetery or their case.

Alex took Spider for a walk. When they came back, Spider was feeling much better.

They soon retired for the night. Alex took out her Bible as Spider fell asleep on his blanket at the foot of the bed.

She read psalm after psalm, praying and reading. Never before had she been forced to deal with something quite like this. She wouldn't try to solve this mystery without definite instructions from the Lord. She believed he would show her the way. She would trust God and proceed through the Holy Spirit's leading.

* * *

On Sunday morning, they went to a local church very close to the bed-and-breakfast. The people were very friendly and welcomed them like they had known them all their lives. The pastor spoke on Psalm 121:

> *I will lift up my eyes to the hills—from whence comes my help? My help comes from the Lord, who made heaven and earth. He will not allow your foot to be moved; He who keeps you will not slumber. Behold, He who keeps Israel shall neither slumber nor sleep. The Lord is your keeper; the Lord is your shade at your right hand. The sun shall not strike you by day, nor the moon by night. The Lord shall preserve you from all evil; He shall preserve your soul. The Lord shall preserve your going out and your coming in from this time forth, and even forevermore.[3]*

Alex liked this psalm very much, and she found that it gave her encouragement for the day ahead.

Ginny was meeting Phil for lunch, so Alex made her way out of town with plans of her own. She had Spider to keep her company. She knew exactly where she was going.

After another hour, she arrived at the cemetery. She followed the tracks from the day before, which were well-indented into the ground by now.

She stopped some distance from where the bodies had been buried and put on her boots. With her gun in her pocket, she left

---

[3] Psalm 121:1–8.

the vehicle with Spider, not on a leash today. The police tape was evident. She walked to where the first cross had been found, then studied each empty grave.

This is crazy, she thought. *What am I doing here?*

It was as if she wanted God to perform some miracle to tell her what to do next. She stood a long time and tried to picture in her mind what the victims had looked like and who they had been. Why had such an awful thing happened to them? Had they all been killed within minutes of each other? Had some of them watched the others die? She shook her head and put her head down. It was too horrible.

While making her way back to the Suburban, she noticed a man walking toward her. She quickly looked for Spider; without having to call him, he came right up to her. He had seen the man too and wasn't sure of him. He let out a deep growl, soft but loud enough to be heard.

The man looked like a farmer, but what did she know about what a farmer looked like these days? He had on light jean overalls and a checkered shirt with the sleeves rolled up.

She took a deep breath and let it out slowly. Was it time to get in her vehicle and drive out of here? Was this man the killer? Maybe the letter writer? Maybe nobody?

"Spider, stay here beside me." The dog moved a tad closer. She could feel his warmth against her leg. She felt his tension. That was all right, under the circumstances.

She was almost to the point of counting the man's steps as he got closer. What should she do? If it was the letter writer, why would he come to her in plain sight? Her hand automatically reached into the pocket of her light jacket where the gun sat nestled, easy to reach if necessary.

He stopped a few paces away. "Excuse me, miss. I mean you no harm. Will that dog bite?" He gave Spider a wary look.

"He will if he thinks I'm threatened in any way." She didn't take her eyes off the man.

"I'm just curious as to what's going on. I live down the way and the phone lines are hopping with questions as to what the police are doing in this cemetery. The people buried here need to be left alone and in peace."

She let out her breath and studied his face, trying to read the man's mind. That was just a crazy thing to do. He didn't look like a killer. But then, she wasn't sure what a killer looked like.

"I'm sorry," she said at last. "I suppose this is normally a quiet place and we're drawing attention to it. We received word that something was going on in the cemetery and we had to check it out. The place isn't looked after back here and we don't want someone to get into an accident. There are sunken graves that need more dirt. Some of the old caskets are practically exposed, without any protection. We decided to contact the police while we were here, just to be safe. The cemetery's caretaker has some workers coming to fix the place up."

She knew the police were sending in lawn mowers today, as well as men to fill in the sunken graves and holes they had left behind. That would make her story look plausible.

"You mean some of the old families want this place cleaned up?" the man asked.

"Wouldn't you, if you had relatives buried here?"

"Yes, I guess so." He shook his head in puzzlement, seeming to doubt her story. He had also noticed the police tape. "But why now?"

At this point, a noise drew their attention. A large dump truck and a couple of mowers were in the process of driving into the cemetery.

"I guess we'd better get out of the way," Alex said. "It was nice meeting you. I didn't get your name."

"Tom Johnston. I still think it's strange, wanting to fix this place after all this time."

She ignored his question and asked one of her own. "Mr. Johnston, have you by any chance noticed anything else unusual in the cemetery lately?"

"If you want to know what's going on around here, try the first farm down the road on the left. White house with bright red shutters. The name Sanders is on the mailbox at the road. Kathy knows all the news and gossip."

"Okay, thanks." She smiled at him and climbed back into her vehicle with Spider sitting right up front.

On her way out of the cemetery, she passed one of the mowers and then made for the road. Through the rear-view mirror, she saw Tom Johnston get into a red truck parked along the side of the road.

"Okay, Spider, here's a question for you," she said as they drove. "Consider the letter writer, the killer, and the surviving daughter. Do you think any of these could live in the house I've just been told about? It's possible, isn't it?"

Alex searched for the white house with bright red shutters and the mailbox. She stopped at the first farm she came to, idling on the shoulder. This could be very dangerous. On the other hand, if she didn't investigate, she wouldn't learn anything new.

She drove up the long, well-worn stone driveway and stopped in front of the farmhouse.

"I need you to stay in the vehicle, Spider." He wasn't fastened in, but the window was down. "Guard her!"

She knew the dog would stay in the front seat unless there was trouble. The dog growled, then let out a bark as if confirming Alex's command.

She made her way to the front door, put her polished fingernail on the buzzer, and pressed. She heard the ring inside the house.

Within a few moments, a woman came to the door. Alex noticed she was dressed quite modernly in jeans and a T-shirt.

"Hi," the woman said. "I bet you're one of the cops checking out the cemetery. The gossipers have been busy with all kinds of thoughts of what we think has happened. Come on in. I've a pot of coffee on."

"Thanks, I'm Alexandria, but everyone just calls me Alex. Are you Kathy Sanders?"

"Yes." The woman led her into a large, modern kitchen. The bright flowered wallpaper caught Alex's eye. "Please, sit down and take a load of your feet."

Kathy poured her a cup of coffee and handed her the sugar and milk pitcher.

"Thank you." Alex didn't see any need to tell the woman she wasn't actually a cop. "I'm sorry to bother you. I was talking to a Mr. Tom Johnston and he told me that you know everything that goes on around here."

"I guess I do, pretty much." She laughed. "Tom Johnston? I can't recall that name."

"He was just in the cemetery. About six feet tall, in his sixties I think. Not bad-looking, with salt-and-pepper hair, deep dark eyes. He was driving a red truck."

"That sounds like one of the Hanselfords. But all the guys around here have red trucks."

Suddenly, a lightbulb went off in Alex's head. That had been one of the names in the letter.

"Did you say Hanselford?"

"Yeah. They're an old family from round here."

Alex paused and lifted her head. "But I'm sure he said Tom Johnston."

"I don't suppose you got a license number or anything like that?"

"No." She frowned and tilted her head with a slight nod, hoping the woman would give her a bit more.

"As far as seeing anything in the cemetery, all the people are dead in there," Kathy said. "Mind you, the people keep it looking nice. Now that I think about it, I did see a red truck there lately. It was about ten in the evening. I was going to retire for the night when I looked out the window and saw a truck sitting out there. I was surprised because the truck's lights went out. I thought it might be dangerous to sit out there without lights, but I just figured it was a couple of lovers. I've seen that same truck there a few times since. It's a red color, almost wine."

"I guess you would know if you had seen it anywhere else in the village…"

"Sorry. There must be hundreds of trucks that color, as I said."

"It sounds like you've lived here for some time," Alex said, pressing on. "You know, I heard there were some suspicions that a family may have been murdered in the country many years ago. Do you remember hearing anything about that?"

"Yeah, our parents and everyone around were scared that some lunatic did it. I think everyone had shotguns at their doors and kept the houses locked up tight for the longest time. Days later, we heard the police were investigating Keith Hanselford, Larry Strandell, and that Wallberry fellow. The next thing we knew, the Williams family had all moved out west and the guys had gone with them. That was all we ever heard of it, and in time everyone just forgot. I went to school with some of the kids in that family."

"Really?" This was getting better every minute, she thought. "Can you remember any of their names or ages?"

"How come the police are so interested in that mess? It was a long time ago."

Alex had to think of an answer quickly. "Sometimes we look back on cold cases. I just heard about it and I'm interested."

Suddenly, Kathy looked toward the window then the door. "Did you hear that? Another car, maybe a truck, just pulled into the driveway. The loose gravel is always a giveaway. And there's a dog barking. Excuse me while I see who it is."

Alex got to her feet, following her. Could the man in the red truck be the letter writer? Curiosity invaded her mind.

"Oh," Kathy said, looking out the window. "It's the chief of police. I guess he's your boss. A real looker, isn't he? I bet the policewomen all like him." She opened the screen door. "Hi, Lorne! I've got one of your detectives here. It sounds to me like you got something going on in the cemetery."

"Hi Kathy." Lorne's face lit up when he spotted Alex beside her. He might have known she would be one step ahead of him. He smiled from one to the other. "Yeah, she's one of my more energetic ladies. She just beat me in coming to see you. Those old phone lines must have been on fire yesterday, and I suppose today."

"Come on in, Lorne. You'll be letting the flies in."

Lorne stepped into the little hallway. He shifted his attention to Alex. "Did you find out what you wanted to know?"

Alex nodded. "You obviously know Mrs. Sanders. She's been wonderful." With some excitement in her voice, she repeated everything Kathy had said about the red truck. "Mrs. Sanders here said that she went to school with some of the Williams kids."

Alex was trying to keep calm, but she was excited about the prospect of finally getting some answers.

Lorne nodded. "Kathy, can you tell us anything else about the family or the kids?"

"Lorne, your friend here said you were looking into an old case," Kathy said. "Don't tell me you're drudging up that Williams thing."

He hesitated. He didn't want word getting out about what they were doing, in case the killer heard the news. That could put him on the offensive and make the investigation more dangerous.

"Kathy, let's go sit down and have a cup of tea," Lorne said. "I need to explain something to you."

"Sure, only coffee." Kathy chuckled. "Who drinks tea anymore?"

Lorne followed the women into the kitchen. Kathy put down a second cup of coffee in front of Alex and then gave one to Lorne as he sat down.

"Kathy, we are looking into that case again," Lorne said as they settled down at the kitchen table. "With the new methods of investigating today, we have some leads. We now believe the family never left but were murdered."

The intake of breath was obvious. Kathy's eyes stared at him, unbelieving.

"In telling you this, Kathy, I'm taking you into my confidence and trust. It is very important that the killer not know we're doing this. He could get vicious if he knew we were after him again. So I need you to keep everything I've said a secret. I know I can count on you." And he smiled at her.

For the first time, Alex noticed how charming he could be. He had Kathy eating right out his hand, listening attentively, taking in every word and gesture.

"Can you remember anything about the family that might help us?" Lorne asked. "Especially the name of older daughter? I heard she was dating some young man."

"Lorne, are you saying I might be in danger?" Kathy asked, ignoring his question.

"No. I just don't want people talking about it. If we can surprise the killer, we have nothing to worry about." Lorne took a sip of coffee. "As far as anyone else is concerned about the cemetery, we made a bust. Some stupid guys were selling and keeping illegal guns." He hesitated, trying to be nice. "Would you remember the names of the family members and their ages?"

Kathy had to pause and go back into her memory.

"Anne was the oldest," she said at last. "I didn't know her all that well, because she wasn't in school anymore. I would say she was probably about twenty at that time. The kids did talk about her and her boyfriend, Marshall Wallberry. Gerald was the next oldest, I think maybe eighteen. Rachel was my age, and we were in the same class. Barbara was next, probably fourteen. Then came Joey, the cutest kid you ever seen, about nine or ten. He was very small for his age with gorgeous bright blue eyes and curly blond hair."

"One other question," Alex said. "Do you know where the Williams farm is located?"

"Sure." She wrote down the directions and left it in the middle of the table.

Alex was so excited that she nearly stopped breathing. She took a deep breath, trying to remain calm. She could hardly contain her enthusiasm at the prospect of going to see the farmhouse. Her whole face lit up.

"Thanks a lot," Lorne said. "You've been a great help, Kathy, and the coffee hit the spot." As he got up, he didn't mention that it had stripped the lining of his stomach. "Please keep this conversation under your hat for now. Do you think I could leave my home phone number with you? If you see that truck again, call me. I don't care what time it is. I'll come and check it out."

Alex pushed her chair back, but before she left she remembered to snatch up the directions Kathy had written down. Then she followed Lorne to the front door. They left the house, thanking Kathy one last time.

All Alex could think about right now was that they finally had names and ages. Now they just needed to know who that red truck belonged to.

They made their way down the driveway, back to their vehicles.

"How did you know where to find me, Chief?" Alex asked. "Are you having me followed?"

"No. I just wanted to make sure the trucks were at the cemetery cleaning up that mess we left, and quickly. My biggest concern is that the killer will soon learn we're reopening the case, and I don't want to give him time to pick up and run if he's still in the country. That's when I recognized your vehicle going up the laneway here." Lorne got into his cruiser and rolled down the window. "Do you want to go see the farmhouse where this all took place?"

"Ohhh…" Alex put a finger to her lips, pretending to be stumped. "I should have written down the directions."

He smiled at her with a glint in his eye. "Too bad."

She laughed, then reached into her pocket and pulled out the directions Kathy had given her and waved the paper at him.

"I'll lead the way," he said with a mischievous glint in his eye.

She shivered with anticipation. Once she was back in the vehicle, she picked up her phone from the seat beside her and called Ginny, hoping she could get Phil to bring her out here to get pictures. She needed pictures.

There was no answer, which meant Ginny was probably out with Phil somewhere. She should have brought Ginny along. But then again, who would ever have thought she would be going to see the Williams house?

CHAPTER EIGHT
THE OLD FARMHOUSE

Alex couldn't hold back her enthusiasm and worry at what they might find at the farmhouse. Thinking about this place and seeing it in person were two wholly different things. There could be absolutely nothing to find there, or it could be covered in dark bloodstains. If so, would the blood be everywhere? Had the family tried to run? Had they died instantly? The father at least had been shot in the head. They knew that now from the coroner.

She started to wonder whether she really wanted to see inside that house. She was glad Lorne would be with her. She wasn't one to believe in ghosts, but it would be a long time before she forgot about her experience in the cemetery. It had only lasted a second, but it had stayed with her.

Alex noticed that Lorne had slowed down just ahead. She did the same. He was obviously looking for the place. Then he seemed to find it and turned down what appeared to have been a laneway once. Now it looked like anything but. Weeds, bushes, and stones covered the path.

"I hope he knows what he's doing," she said to Spider, glad he was secured in his harness. The lane was bumpy, and in some places the earth dropped into ruts and holes. Both sides of the roadway, if one could call it that, were overgrown. Strings of ivy had smothered the trees to death.

They had to travel slowly and she was glad she had a good, powerful vehicle.

When they came to the end of the lane, she peered straight out the windshield.

"Well, Spider, we're here." The house was such a sad sight, forgotten and forsaken. She almost wanted to cry. What had at one time been a lovely whitewashed house had turned a dirty gray, with most of the paint gone. The trim had lost all its paint, windows once bright with sunlight were obscured by panes of glass streaked from the elements, and the upstairs window curtains had been torn. Some of the windows were covered with plywood where glass had been broken. The windows and front door where boarded up.

She parked her Suburban and climbed out just as Lorne did the same.

"Is it safe to let Spider out?" she called to him.

"Yes, but keep him on a tight leash until we know what we have here. I have no idea what's around the place."

She did as he said, with a lot of apprehension. Together they walked toward the house.

"Spider, we'll need your good nose," Lorne said as he leaned over and rubbed the dog's ears. "Let me know if you smell any danger."

Alex was pleased they were getting along so well.

"Well, this is it." He stared at the house. "You know, I think some of you is washing off on me. I've never had a great imagination, but you've got me thinking. I wonder if maybe that Wallberry guy came back here to live with the girl—well, she'd be a woman now. If that was the case, he wouldn't want anyone coming around, so he might leave the place in disrepair."

"I think we had better go slow and careful," she said in agreement.

He nodded. "I've left a message for Phil to meet us her. He probably has Virginia with him. I should have had a couple of my guys meet us here. I don't suppose you have a gun or a license to carry."

"I do, actually." She smiled and patted her pocket. "Force of habit when I'm away from home in a strange place. I don't think the killer would come back here, even if he heard you had reopened the case up again. If he knew, I think he'd run as far as he could get." She turned her eyes back on the ruined home. "It's sad, isn't it?"

A forlorn frown went with her words. She remembered a few words from a poem she had read somewhere: *Just one life, 'twill soon be passed, only what's done for Christ will last.*

"If I can get some of the boards off, do you want to go inside?" Lorne asked.

"Do you?" She smiled at him.

"Yes, of course. I'm as curious as you are."

She paused, feeling a touch of fear and dread. She had to remind herself that this was part of her job as a reporter. She walked toward the house with trepidation, her heart beating faster. Spider stayed right at her side, as if knowing these weren't normal circumstances. He could probably feel her tension.

"Let's check the outside first," Lorne said.

They took their time walking around the house. It was a good size, large enough to fit a big family. She noticed a spacious sunroom that must have been nice in its day. It all looked so sad and neglected now.

"We will need tools to get in this house," he said. The wood boards were well nailed on.

At the back, they found a shed-like structure joined to the back door, probably to keep the cold out in winter months. A good-sized shed and a couple of henhouses rose from the far side of the yard, with a large barn towards the back of the property.

"Let's have a look in the outbuildings first," Lorne suggested. "I'd like to make sure they're empty. Do you mind the walk? Spider would obviously like it."

"That will be fine." She was anxious to go inside these structures.

For a man she didn't know, she liked Lorne. He seemed to be kind, and he really liked Spider; that was more than a plus. He didn't have that hurry-hurry attitude she saw in everyone back home either.

Lorne first went inside the shed that probably had housed farm equipment at one time. It was empty now. Next came the henhouses. He ducked so he didn't hit his head on the low roof. He found them empty too, but the smell of chickens still lingered in the place. He supposed people not used to farms noticed these smells more others.

He checked the other two shacks, and they were empty too.

"I suppose if people thought they moved, someone must have taken the livestock," he said.

"Maybe it was Marshall Wallberry," Alex suggested. "Or whoever killed them?"

A murmur of possible agreement came from Lorne's lips. His eyes went to the barn still several feet away.

"I'd like to look in the barn," he said.

"Okay, Spider and I are right with you."

They walked toward the barn on an old worn path which was overrun with weeds. When a rut caught Alex's foot, she grabbed for Lorne for help. Their faces came very close, and their eyes almost spoke to each other for an embarrassing moment. They burst out laughing. Even Spider had a few barks, not wanting to be left out. He got his ears rubbed and was getting spoiled by this likeable stranger.

"Excuse me. Are we missing something here?" Ginny's voice echoed right behind them. "I know I should have stayed in the car, but when Phil saw you walking out here, he said I better come with him."

"I didn't want to leave her back there alone," Phil said as the two newcomers came around the side of the house into the back yard. He was surprised by what he saw; that had looked like a kiss! This wasn't like Lorne, and he didn't think Alex was his type. Lots of single girls were just waiting for a chance to hook up with him. As far as he was concerned, Lorne was too fussy. "I have a crew coming. I hope that's all right. I figured you would consider it a crime scene now."

"Good," Lorne said as he broke free from Alex. "We're going to need to get those boards removed. I want to check out the barn first, though. You might as well come with us."

They carried on walking. The nearer they got, Alex noticed a strange smell in the air that was hard to describe. A bit repugnant, nothing she could describe, but it was there.

Ginny wrinkled her nose, noticing it too.

"That isn't a skunk," Lorne said to Alex. "I think you'd better stay here while we go and see what it is."

"Lorne, it couldn't be dead animals after all this time," Phil said. He puckered his nose and turned up his lips.

Lorne kept approaching the barn. "Ladies, just stay here."

Spider tried to pull away from her to follow Lorne, and it was all Alex could do to keep him at her side.

"Spider, stop that!" she said. He listened for about a second, but then started pulling at her again. "Spider! Stop that right now. Sit!"

He finally sat, but she could tell he didn't want to. She had never seen that in him before.

Before Lorne reached the barn, he noticed a pigpen attached to the far side. The fence around it had partially collapsed. Not surprising, considering how much time had passed.

Phil and he walked closer to examine it.

"The fence is constructed of heavy gage steel mesh," Phil pointed out.

Lorne examined it and noticed that the fence had been cut. "Whoever did this would have needed heavy-duty wire cutters. Why would anyone take the pigs out this way, since there's a proper exit nearer the back? I wouldn't want the pigpen entrance next to the barn door."

"I don't know, but the odor isn't coming from the pigpen." Phil took a few steps to the large barn door and realized that the weird smell was obviously coming from inside, seeping out through the crack under the door. He had to tug at the door before it opened.

Both men stood a second for going inside.

Tons of flies hovered over a space a few feet from them, near the floor. They almost swarmed out the door from the gush of air that had rushed in.

At first, they didn't know what they were looking at. Then Lorne saw a mess of bones, almost in a heap. It was a dreadful sight. He couldn't believe his eyes. Phil just swatted at the flies still fluttering about where he stood.

"Lorne, they must have left some the animals to starve to death."

"It would appear that way." He stuck the toe of his boot against the of a skull. "Look at the flat nose bone!"

It was the skull of a huge hog.

Lorne walked around and soon noticed cattle skulls too. The weird smell coming from the pile was impossible to imagine, probably because the barn had no open windows for the odors to escape over time. The bloodstains had turned brownish-red, seeping into the wooden floor and leaving their own odor of decay.

Getting used to the smell, Lorne kicked at the pile with his boot to move some bones out of the way and determine what they were exactly. He supposed some of these animals had been eaten by their own, to avoid starvation. He would have to call animal control to come and clean up the remains.

Outside, Alex couldn't stand the wait any longer and walked into the barn. She wasn't going to hold her nose, either.

Just bite the bullet, she told herself. *Pretend you don't even notice it.*

It wasn't easy but she did it, moving next to Lorne and Phil. She stopped and gawked at the pile of bones. For a moment, she wasn't sure what she was looking at.

"I don't think you want to see this, Alex," Lorne said.

"Bones," she said. "Surely animal bones. Lorne, this is terrible. What kind of person would do this?" It didn't seem real. "Do you mind if I get Ginny to take some pictures?"

"You're sure you want pictures of this?" Lorne asked.

She wanted to argue, but then she thought better. Ginny probably couldn't do handle this. It was hardly the fashion section.

"I'll see you get some photos," Lorne said. "My photographer will get some for us both. Come on, we've seen enough."

She turned and left, with the guys followed her. They left the doors open as they emerged into the yard.

Ginny was having trouble controlling Spider.

"What's inside?" Ginny asked, peering around the guys.

"Nothing much," she said. "Just some old bones."

She didn't see the amusement expressed on Lorne's face.

"No wonder you wanted to see what's in there, Spider," Lorne said. "Keep a hold on him, Virginia. There's way too much for him to get into here."

Lorne couldn't figure out why the farmer had put the pigs in the barn with the other animals. It must have been obvious to them what would happen if those animals were left alone. For that matter, if the farmer had been any good, he should have had more animals than the remains indicated.

"Alex, I would feel better if you fastened the dog outside the house," Lorne said. "Give him lots of rope and he'll have a good time."

She did as he suggested, glad that he was still willing to include her in the investigation. He could have shut her down a long time ago.

They heard the sound of cars coming down the laneway. Alex saw that they were police cruisers.

"Our guys," Phil said. "I'll get them to take down the boards as soon as they can."

"Tell them to start with the doors," Lorne said. "I want to go in through the back door. Get the officer with the camera to capture everything he can. I want the whole place photographed." He turned to Alex. "Are you ready to see inside the house?"

She nodded reluctantly. The bones had upset her more than she let on.

They waited for some officers to remove the boards from the back door. Once it was clear, Lorne tried the handle and found it locked. He pulled a tiny screwdriver from his belt.

"I hate breaking down doors like they do on television," he said, chuckling.

It only took a moment to fiddle with the lock.

"If I can have your attention for a minute, everyone," Lorne announced to everyone present once the door was unlocked. "I want to walk through the house. Then you're free to go in and set up your equipment—and don't miss anything. We're after a person who killed seven or eight people, and it's our job to get him."

He went on giving orders for several minutes in regards to the house.

Once finished, he turned to Alex and Ginny. "Put on these gloves and try not to touch anything. Just look."

He walked in and held the door for the other three to follow.

Inside, they found themselves in the back shed. If it was like most farmhouses, Alex expected it would probably lead into the kitchen. She kept her eyes down, watching her feet. It was fairly dark.

"Look at that!" Ginny pointed to the row shoes on the floor. "Oh Alex, they're shoes. The family must have left them here." She made a grimace at the thick grey clumps of dust abiding in each shoe, along with strings of cobwebs.

"Are you sure you want to go on?" Alex said quietly to her. "You can stay out here if you want."

"Then who would get your pictures?" She pointed her camera at the shoes and the flash went off.

"Yes, but it's so awful."

Alex noticed several hooks on the wall with jackets hanging off them. The jackets all looked the same, dulled by time and now covered in thick grey dust that made them appear almost ghost-like. A shiver ran down her spine.

Lorne walked up to the door leading into the main house and she followed. Her legs felt shaky with nerves.

They entered a large kitchen. Lorne touched the light switch, but of course there was no power.

He turned to Phil. "Call Miller and tell him we need Hydro out here like yesterday."

"Yes, sir." Phil quickly left the house.

They stood rooted to the spot, feeling like they were intruding on something sacred.

Alex wasn't sure what she was doing here. It was almost like she expected to see the terrible thing that had happened replay before her eyes.

It was a typical old farmhouse kitchen, although it had a rather modern stove and refrigerator for the time the occupants had lived here. They'd also had modern plumbing. They obviously hadn't been poor farmers. With every step they took, a halo of dust rose from their feet. They all sneezed, the sounds echoing off the walls.

"What do you think?" Lorne said as he stepped in front of the refrigerator, looking at Alex.

"Probably full of bad food. After all, who would take the stuff out?" Her face screwed up, expecting the worse.

He opened the fridge, and a nasty odor attacked them again. Although empty, it had not been cleaned.

The stovetop was still covered with pots and pans, as well as food that had gone to mildew. Someone had prepared a meal but never eaten it. Alex grabbed her stomach and moved away as a flash bulb went off. She wondered how much worse it could get. She had to keep reminding herself that this family had died fifteen years ago.

"Not a scrap of food." Lorne shook his head in surprise as he looked through the cupboards. "Okay, Miss Reporter, what do you think of that?"

"I think we're looking at the boyfriend again, that he and the girl took the food with them. Who knows? Maybe he took some of the livestock too. Maybe he had a truck and only so much room."

Lorne nodded. "Especially if the girl went willingly."

She shook her head unbelieving. "So you're thinking she's as guilty as he is?"

"I don't think we can assume anything until we know more facts. I suppose if the killer had to hide out with the girl, they would need every bit of food they could get. I have to say, this doesn't look good for the girl."

"He could have forced her to empty the cupboards," Alex pointed out. "She might not have even been aware of what she was doing, not if she had just witnessed him kill her family."

"I suppose we might never know the answer to that question—unless we find her."

Alex noticed that there was no dining room, just a huge table with ten chairs seated around it. The table had been set for ten, although it was obvious no one had eaten anything. The dishes were clean with the exception of a couple inches of dust shaped like balloons.

Ginny was doing her job, and finding it far more interesting and exciting than anything she had ever shot before. Every time a flash went off, they all got a better view of everything around them.

Phil returned in a hurry. "Hydro is here. They were working on a farm just down the road. We'll have power within the next half-hour."

"That will be a big help. Thanks, Phil."

Phil made his way to where Ginny was taking pictures. She quickly snapped a couple of him and smiled. Then she went back to work.

"Ten chairs," Lorne said with a puzzled look on his face. "Maybe they were expecting three guests for dinner."

"It looks like the food on the stove was ready to go to the table," Alex surmised. "Did an argument lead to the killing before they had time to eat? The killer could have been one of the guests. But why? All we really know is that there are seven graves in that cemetery."

Next, Lorne noticed more chairs sitting here and there around the edges of the room, as well as a pullout couch and a couple of easy chairs. It was obvious the family had done a lot of living in this room. The kitchen and dining room seemed to have doubled as a family room.

"Okay, let's continue our tour." But Lorne wasn't sure where to go next. There were three open doors, one closed, and an archway into a parlor. One of the doors led upstairs. The second revealed a small washroom, and the third opened into the sunroom. The closed door led to the basement.

They decided to go through the arch into the parlor, but they stopped just inside the door. Suddenly the whole place lit up. The hydro had kicked in.

"Apparently no one turned out the lights," Phil said. They stared as dark-brown stains showing through the flower-patterned rug. "If you didn't know what happened here, you might not notice the blood under this blanket of dust."

Lorne circled the parlor a few times, dodging furniture. Ginny followed him, taking pictures. Another officer with a camera appeared at the door. With two cameras going off, it was like a bad lightning storm.

Alex stayed put near the door, not wanting to get in the way.

"There are three pools of blood," Lorne said. "The killer must have stood right where I am, and shot—one, two, and three—all in a matter of seconds. Where do you suppose the others were?"

Alex turned, not wanting to stay in the parlor. It could have been her imagination, but she had a funny feeling about it. Cold, icy dampness and wisps of dust danced in the air as the cameras flashed.

"There's a sunroom off the kitchen we still haven't checked, as well as upstairs," she murmured.

"Go ahead," Lorne told her. "Just don't touch anything. I'll be right there."

Ginny was so into her pictures she had forgotten everything else going on around her. Alex was surprised she was so good at her job.

Alex made her way to the sunroom. She opened the door and stared inside. The room contained an old computer and a large television. It only took her second to guess that if the adult guests had been in the parlor, the children might have been in here.

"Lorne," she called. "Come here."

Lorne stepped into the doorway behind her.

"The youngest members of the family were probably in here," she said. Alex's eyes searched the floor. She found four pools of dried blood. "Look at the bloodstains."

He moved about the room, carefully looked the space over. "You're right. Four people were killed in this room. Four in the parlor, and three in here. Seven total. So who buried them in the cemetery?"

"Obviously the killer."

"But what happened to the three guests? By all appearances, the family was entertaining. We also have to consider the three men named in the letter. The killer might have been a dinner guest…"

"I'd like to look upstairs," Alex said. "Do you want to come with me?"

"No, you go ahead. Ginny will follow you. I want to see the basement."

Alex made her way up the stairs, which were closed in on both sides. The first bedroom she came to the door was wide open. It had a double bed with a lovey handmade quilt.

"This must have been the parents' room," she said to Ginny, who kept snapping pictures. Alex opened a closet door. "It's full of their clothes."

"That's not surprising," Ginny said. "The killer wouldn't have wanted their clothes. I guess we can rule out the parents."

The oldest daughter's room had what had been very pretty paper on the walls, with tiny roses all over it, and a gorgeous quilt on the single bed. Alex opened the closet door, expecting to find it empty. It wasn't.

"There goes your theory that the oldest daughter is still alive," Ginny said, smiling. "If she left with her boyfriend, she would have taken her clothes with her."

"It's getting more complicated all the time."

Together, they moved further down the hall, looking from room to room, always finding the same thing—the closets full of clothes.

The last room along the hall contained lots of stuffed animals. The kid who lived here must have loved teddy bears, and the wallpaper verified this. There was an old rocking hose, and several toy trucks and cars. Alex didn't want to go into this room. For some reason she couldn't.

"Don't worry about pictures in here," Alex said. "I've seen enough. This is going to be one of the most difficult stories I've ever written. I hope James appreciates what it's doing to me."

"I called him earlier to give him an update. He seemed okay with everything that's going on."

"Thank you." Alex turned to go back down the stairs.

Before they got to the stairs, however, Lorne walked up and met her.

"There's nothing unusual in the basement," he said as two detectives passed them, heading up. "They're going to work up here. Did you check the closets? Were any empty?"

"No," Alex said. "There goes our theory about the oldest girl."

Alex and Ginny went back downstairs, meeting Phil in the kitchen.

"Where's Lorne?" Phil asked. His face had a look of dismay, even anger.

"He's upstairs," Alex answered, thinking he sounded abrupt and didn't look like his normal self.

"Lorne!" Phil hollered up the stairs. "We need you to come to the barn right away."

"Coming," Lorne called back, noting the urgency in the detective's voice.

Alex walked out of the house and into the back yard, looking toward the barn. Everything looked all right to her. But Lorne and Phil ran past her, heading for the barn.

Twenty whole minutes later, the two men came out again. She noticed that neither man seemed to be in a hurry. Lorne had the same haunted, angry look she'd seen on Phil.

"I've just called the coroner," Lorne said, sighing. "One of my guys has some emergency medical training. She thinks there are some human bones, and possibly a human skull among the dead animals."

"Oh no, Lorne. That's awful." Alex couldn't stop herself from picturing an animal feeding on a dead person. She gagged, her hand going to her stomach. She gulped, hoping she wouldn't throw up.

Ginny, too, put her hand on her forehead and closed her eyes. She didn't want to let her imagination go wild.

"That answers what happened to the others," Lorne said. "The killer obviously figured no one would find the bones in the barn. They were left there for the animals to feast on." He put his hands in his pockets. "We'll see what Luke thinks. I'm going to wait for him. Alex, do you want to stay or go? I'll understand either way."

She smiled encouragingly. "I'm staying."

Phil made his way back to the house where they were working to gather evidence.

CHAPTER NINE
PEOPLE FROM THE PAST

Lorne called the animal control people, and when they arrived the man in charge confirmed that there were more than animal bones in the barn. He believed some were human. Luke soon arrived, and Lorne took him to the barn as well.

A short time later, Luke emerged and joined Alex and Lorne in the yard.

"Well, Chief, there must be quite a story here," Luke said. "We have the bones of one person in there. I'm fairly sure he was male and that he was shot. Whoever's responsible for this must have been completely out of their mind. The only good thing any about this is that he was at least dead before… well, you know." He looked shaken by the discovery. "My guys will take the human remains to the morgue. We may never be able to figure out who he was."

"Thanks, Luke," Lorne said. "I appreciate your help. If you do find out anything, please let me know."

Lorne and Alex watched the gurney leave the barn with the bones lying atop it in a heap. Animal control finished up their work and left a short time later.

Alex turned away. She didn't want to be a part of this.

When the gurneys were gone and she looked behind her, she saw Lorne playing in the yard with Spider. They were having a ball. Lorne was so good with him that she worried she might have lost the dog to another.

Lorne stopped when he noticed her looking. "In case you're worrying about your friend, Phil is keeping her busy. She has some amazing pictures for you! Anyway, they left a little while ago. Virginia said she would see you later." He smiled at Alex, liking her more all the time. "Let's get out of here. Would you like to come with me?"

"Yes, I would."

She knew she was in trouble when it came to Lorne. She was becoming very fond of him. Dare she think about the word love? No, they didn't even know one another.

God, what is going on between us? Neither of us need to be hurt.

"We should check to see if Marshall has any surviving family at the last address we have for him," Lorne continued. "And I want to try and find his friends, Larry Strandell and Keith Hanselford. If we can find them, that is."

They walked around the house to the front yard.

"The address we have for Marshall is in Welland," Lorne said as they approached their vehicles. "We might as well go together in my car. I'll have one of my officers take your Suburban back to the bed-and-breakfast."

They got into Lorne's police cruiser and left the old farmhouse. It was a fair trip to get to Welland, although it was a nice drive and Alex enjoyed the company. She enjoyed the smell of his aftershave.

The time passed quickly, although they traveled in silence, neither knowing what to say. They had so much on their minds that they couldn't think straight. There were so many unanswered questions.

When they arrived at the address, they remained in the car, looking at the modest home in a poor area of the city. It was an original wartime house that had been remodeled a few times.

"You don't have to come with me, you know," Lorne said. "Unless you want to."

"Thanks, I know that. I want to go."

They walked side by side up to the small porch. Lorne rang the doorbell and they waited, not sure what to expect. They both felt anxious.

A young woman came to the door. She was about five-foot-six and dressed in jeans, an orange T-shirt, and flats on her feet.

"I'm sorry to bother you, ma'am," Lorne said. "I'm Lorne Merritt, chief of police in St. Catharines. I'm looking for a member of the Wallberry family."

"I'm Samantha," she said. "Marshall's cousin."

"May we come in and talk with you for a few minutes? It's very important."

"Sure, why not?" She looked at them warily, having no idea what they wanted. "Do you want a cup of tea?"

"No, ma'am, just a few minutes of your time."

"Come in and sit down."

Samantha ushered them into a nice, homey living room. It looked well lived in, with newspapers scattered about and a couple of books lying open on the coffee table.

"I'm looking for Marshall Wallberry," Lorne said. "Does he live here?"

"Are you kidding?" Samantha asked. "Not for years! Goodness, that must be... let me see, about twelve or fifteen years ago. He just up and left town with his two friends—that judge's son, Larry something-or-other, and the Hanselford kid. I figured they got into some kind of trouble. I have no idea where any of them are."

"Did you ever hear Marshall talk about a young woman by the name of Anne Williams?"

"Yes. Marshall was dating her at one time. It was so long ago. I'm sorry, I don't remember much about it. I really can't help you."

"Okay, thank you so much."

Lorne and Alex got up and left the house, making their way back to the police cruiser.

"She really wasn't much help," he said, sounding discouraged. "Let's try the Strandell house. We're not far. The family lives on the edge of town, in one of the wealthier neighborhoods. Are you up for that?"

"Sure, only I need a bite to eat. What would you say to getting takeout and eating on the way?"

"I know just the place. You've never tasted hotdogs like these. They have foot-long homemade rolls and twenty-four different toppings. They cook the wieners in some kind of broth, and they're habit-forming. I go once a week."

"That sounds like fun!"

They went to a roadside stand and sat on the patio, eating hotdogs. She had put on four different relishes, three mustards, tomatoes, warm beans, sauerkraut, and several pickles.

They ate, laughed, and ended up with more topping on them than on the hotdogs. Afterward she was so full that she could hardly move, although she had enjoyed every minute. She washed it down with a homemade iced green tea.

"In the winter, they replace the cold relishes with hot ingredients like tiny fried potatoes and onions, even kernels of corn," he said, smiling warmly.

Once they had cleaned up, they got back in the car and drove to the Strandell house.

"Let's go in and see what we have here," Lorne said.

He pulled up into the driveway then walked up onto the veranda where they found three wicker armchairs with flowered padded cushions seats and backs. The color matched the pinks and reds of the wreath on the door. The glass in the window, etched with leaves, was gorgeous. This was the sort of house most people dreamed of owning but never would.

They hadn't even rung the doorbell when an older man swung the door open. Alex guessed that he was around sixty-five, maybe nearer to seventy. He was tall and had a good head of dark, almost black hair with a touch of grey at the temples that gave him a sophisticated look. He was well dressed and wore leather loafers that must have cost a bundle. He was really very good-looking for an older man.

"Are you the police?" The man stared at them.

"Yes." Lorne smiled. "How are you today, Judge?"

"I'm fine." Judge Strandell recognized Lorne, but not the woman with him.

"Were you expecting me?"

"No. I was walking past the window when I saw you pull into my driveway. I can spot the police right off."

Keep calm, stay cool, the judge told himself. He had heard that the police were reopening the Williams case. *Why now after all this time? Just play dumb. No one can prove Larry had anything to do with that.*

"I'm Chief Lorne Merritt from the St. Catharines Police Department. This is my partner for the day, Alexandria. I'm sorry to bother you. I'm looking for Larry Strandell. I believe he's your son, as well as Marshall Wallberry and Keith Hanselford."

"Yes, I'm Larry's father. Please come in."

They walked in and stood just inside the door. He had no intention of asking them any farther into his house. He didn't want them here at all.

"Larry lives out west," the judge said. "He's lived in Vancouver for years and is doing very well. He's a top-notch lawyer, you know."

Just then, a woman appeared in the hallway.

"Who are our guests?" the newcomer asked. "Surely you can invite them into the living room, dear. Please, come in and make yourselves comfortable. Can I get you something to drink?" They sat down on the beige damask chesterfield.

"No thank you." Lorne felt something wrong between these two; the judge's expression was not a happy one.

"It sounded like you were talking about Larry," the woman said. Lorne assume it must be the judge's wife. Alarm was written on her face. "Nothing has happened to him, has it?"

"No, of course not," the judge said. "It's the police and they're looking for some of his old friends."

Lorne made eye contact with the woman. "We're looking for Marshall Wallberry, Keith Hanselford, and your son, Mrs. Strandell."

"Oh, Larry lives out west and he's doing ever so well. We are very proud of him."

"My poor wife has never been able to get over his moving away. He just up and left without telling us, you see." The judge shook his head as if he still couldn't believe it. "He called me much later to tell me he was fine. I just hope he'll come home one day and all will be forgiven."

"When did you say this happened?" Lorne asked.

"I didn't actually. But it was the middle of July, near as I can remember."

Mrs. Strandell sighed, giving him a disgusted glance. "Oh Marvin, it was early July when Larry left. You just can't imagine how worried I was. It must have been early September when he finally phoned you. I remember the day well. I was both happy and sad—happy to hear he was well, and sad that he hadn't called in the evening so I could talk to him too." She turned abruptly, sat down in a chair, and stared at the judge.

They all looked at him at the same time. Then, just as quickly, she stood up again and walked toward her husband.

"This is your fault, Marvin," she said. "He was your son and you didn't understand him. And that girl… you didn't like her either."

It's a good thing looks can't kill, Lorne thought, narrowing his eyes at the mention of a girl.

"Judge, I'm not changing the subject, but you have me slightly confused," Lorne said. "We're investigating the murder of a family by the name of Williams fifteen years ago."

Suddenly Lorne's travel phone went off. He picked up the awkward thing from his pocket.

"Excuse me please." He pressed a button. "Yes?"

"It's Luke from the coroner's office. We have identified the man from the barn using dental records. His name is Marshall Wallberry. He was shot and had bullet fragments in his ribcage. That's the best I can do."

"Thank you. I'll talk to you later." Lorne put the phone back in his pocket and then looked from Alex to the judge. "Judge, if I understand you, you're saying that your son is living in Vancouver?"

"Yes. We get letters from him all the time.

"May I see one?"

"I'm sorry, but I throw them out after we read them. My wife still misses him, and they are a reminder."

"Well, thank you both for your help," Lorne said. "We'll be in touch."

He and Alex both got up and left. As they walked out of the house, Alex noticed that the judge's wife kept nattering at him. She was very unhappy with her husband.

"Lorne, it would be interesting to be a fly on the wall after we left."

He glanced in her direction and smiled.

"You know what I think?" Alex said when they were back in the vehicle. "You should do some checking up on that judge. I felt he was hiding something."

"I will. By the way, that call was from Luke. We've identified the bones of the man in the barn. It was Marshall Wallberry."

"Really? Well, that makes things even more complicated. Are you satisfied the judge's son is out west?"

"No. Until we identify those bodies from the cemetery, we won't know for sure who we're looking for. But we can rule out Wallberry."

On the way back to St. Catharines, they stopped at a restaurant and had a nice buffet dinner. They talked for a long time, getting to know one another better and enjoying the evening. Then he took her back to the bed-and-breakfast.

CHAPTER TEN
THE PHONE CALL

Alex got ready for bed. Spider had already curled up on the bed, tired from his busy day, when she heard a knock on her door.

"May I come in?" the bed-and-breakfast owner asked. "I'm sorry to bother you. I have a man on the phone downstairs asking for the lady reporter. He says that he needs to talk to you and that it's very important. He's called three times in the last hour."

"Okay, I'll come down and get it," Alex said. She couldn't imagine who it would be. She had called James, just as he'd asked her to, that morning. There wasn't much she could keep from him, even telephone numbers.

Alex followed the owner to the front hallway and picked up the phone off its stand.

"Hello," she said.

"Is this the woman reporter from out of town?" The voice sounded strange, like someone with a bad cold, low and wispy.

"Yes, it is," she answered, puzzled. It definitely wasn't James.

"Miss, I made a huge mistake in writing you that letter. It backfired on me. I believed it would solve a lot of problems, but it hasn't. Please just drop it and go home. Forget you ever received that letter, and I'm sorry it brought your mother into the equation.

Get out while you can and let the police handle it. You may even be putting yourself in danger."

The line went dead. Alex stood looking at the phone, not sure if that had been a threat. She didn't like this one bit. She had to tell Lorne.

She pulled picked up the phone from its cradle again and dialled his number.

Lorne answered on the third ring. "Does this mean you can't live without me?" he asked, chuckling.

"Maybe." She told him exactly what had happened.

"Well, I'm sure you're safe for tonight. By the way, you're not going home unless you want to. As far as your mother is concerned, maybe we can go talk to her together. I do have a problem with you staying at the bed-and-breakfast, though. I would rather know you're somewhere safe and out of the killer's way. Would you consider coming to stay with me? Strictly business. That way I'll know what's going on. I can bug the phones and have more control over what's happening. There's lots of room for you both, and Spider too. I can't expect the woman who owns that bed-and- breakfast to put up with cops all over the place."

She could just imagine the frown on his face while saying that. She had to admit that she liked this man very much.

"Do you really have room for three more?" Alex asked. "I mean, are you sure?"

She had no idea what Ginny might think about this. Would the Lord agree with it? She would never do anything to put a question to her being a child of the Lord.

"Yes, I do," he said with a laugh. "Spider, Ginny, and you. I live in a good-sized house, and I have a gem of a housekeeper. She even has a sister to lend a hand. My brother is staying with me too, but I'm not sure for how long. He comes and goes. I'm sure he'll keep out of your way. I can't guarantee he'll stay out of Ginny's way, though."

"Well, Ginny seems to have an interest in Phil right now," Alex said. "She had a dinner date with him tonight." She was glad of the two were interested in each other. It meant she didn't have to worry about Ginny.

"Really? Phil is a nice guy." Lorne laughed. "Can you pack your things and be ready first thing in the morning? I'll tell Alice that you're coming." He paused. "No, wait a minute. I'm swamped with work right now. I'll give you the address. Please, just make your way there whenever you're ready." He gave her directions.

She was surprised to discover that he actually lived in Niagara-on-the-Lake. She was familiar with the lovely homes there, and it would be a pleasure to stay in one of them. It was her favorite part of the country.

She made her way back to the bedroom, with Ginny in her thoughts. She wanted more than anything to do what the Lord wanted her to do. She read Romans 8 in her Bible; she had a marker there and had read it many times. It had some special verses that always seemed to speak to her.

She read it twice and then ended up reading out loud. "Yet in all these things we are more than conquerors through Him who loved us. For I am persuaded that neither death nor life, nor angels nor principalities nor powers, nor things present nor things to come, nor height nor depth, nor any other created thing, shall be able to separate us from the love of God which is in Christ Jesus our Lord."[4]

Her prayers took much longer this night, with so much to talk to the Lord about. She knew he was aware of all she had gone through. She believed that he had brought her here, so she talked to him as though he was right there in the room with her. She

---

[4] Romans 8:37–39.

often felt like she could almost reach out and feel the hand of the Lord as he took her hand in his.

The next morning, after a lot of struggle, she woke Ginny early.

"Wake up, sleepyhead," she said. "I have some things I have to talk to you about."

"I'm so tired. Can't it wait until later? Say, ten o'clock?" Ginny pulled the sheet up to her neck.

"Come on, it's important. We're going to move so Lorne and I can work the case together. He has a large house and has lots of room for us. He also feels it's an imposition for the owner here to have cops around all the time."

Ginny jumped up in bed, sitting straight up. "You're kidding! At Lorne's place? Wait a minute. Is there something going on between you too? Not that I would mind, but I don't want to see you hurt. He's too good-looking not to have strings attached somewhere, you know."

"It's nothing like that, I can assure you. It's strictly business. Now, I need you to get your things packed so we can drive to his place." She didn't want to say anything about the phone call. It would only worry her.

"Okay, I'll have a shower and get dressed."

After breakfast, Alex paid the lady for their stay. An hour later they were in the car, driving toward Niagara.

"Isn't this where we were going for that holiday?" Ginny asked.

"Yes. I need to make a stop first, so you might as well meet my parents. They live in Niagara Falls, away from the hubbub. But then we'll carry on to Niagara-on-the-Lake." She decided to call Lorne about their plans. She hoped he would understand.

"What does that mean? Dare I ask?"

"Hold on." She took out her phone, dialed, and put it to her ear.

"Good morning, Alex," Lorne answered. "How are you this morning? Are you on your way to my place?"

"Sort of. I'm going to make a stop first," she said. "I told you that my parents live in the neighborhood, right? I'm going to drop by and talk to them again now that I know so much more about what happened to the Williams family." She paused. "We can still go to a hotel if that would be better for you."

"I wouldn't have asked you if I didn't want you to stay with me." He laughed. "And yes, I'm well aware of your family and where they live. I looked into them when their names came up in the case."

She kept her eyes on the road. "Just as soon as I leave my parents, I'll pass go and go directly your place." She chuckled. "See you."

She hung up and put the phone down.

"You know I'm not a guy person, Ginny. Common sense tells me I shouldn't, but I really like this guy. There's something special about him. I can't quite put my finger on it. He's warmhearted and kind to us, considering we're the interlopers."

"So it would seem. This guy may be too good to be true, though. Take it easy or you'll end up with a broken heart. Believe me. I know what I'm talking about."

"And are you taking the same advice with Phil?"

"You can believe it. We're having a good time, but we're just friends. We both know this isn't going anywhere. I know he's keeping me out of his boss's way, and that's all right."

They traveled some distance and finally stopped at a large, beautiful home just outside the city of Niagara Falls.

"So you were born in this gorgeous country," Ginny marveled as they got out of the Suburban.

"More or less. In a small place called Dunnville, but I especially love Niagara Falls and Niagara-on-the-Lake. It is touristy, but that doesn't bother me. I guess this area will always feel like home."

I hope they're not surprised to see me, she thought as they drove right into the driveway.

They left the vehicle, Ginny following Alex up some steps to a large wooden veranda. There was a white wicker small round table between two matching chairs.

Alex knocked on the door and it was almost immediately opened. Her mother took Alex in her arms and gave her a big hug.

"I knew you would come after that phone call a few days ago," her mother said. "Oh, Alex, why can't people mind their own business?"

Her father appeared next and did the same, giving her a hug and a kiss on the cheek. "My dear, what a surprise! Aren't you coming back in just a couple of weeks for your holiday? Of course, it's good to see you no matter when you come."

Suddenly both pairs of eyes went to the attractive young woman with Alex.

"Dad, Mom, this is Ginny, and Spider is out in the car. I didn't bring him in, as we can't stay. We're on our way to Niagara-on-the-Lake for some work. Anyway, I didn't want to cause you any unexpected problems."

"Oh, Alex, you would never do that," her mother said.

Alex introduced them. "Ginny, meet my father, Stanley Rutherford, and my mom Jessica."

"It's nice to meet you, Ginny," Stanley said. "Come in and sit down. At least have a cup of coffee."

They entered the front room and slipped their shoes off, not to soil the thick luscious carpet.

"Ginny, it's nice to meet you," Jessica said. "I'm glad my daughter isn't traveling about alone. She seems to forget that life can be dangerous. She promised her father that being a reporter wouldn't be dangerous, or she wouldn't have taken the job. Her father worries about her."

"Of which I have told him dozens of time, there is no need." She cast a glance at her father. She'd made that promise back when he'd had his heart attack and she was just starting her career. He was well now.

"I'm pleased to meet you," Ginny said, thinking Jessica's comments were a bit funny. After all, Alex worked with danger every day.

They sat down in the family room and were soon served coffee and some cheese on biscuits.

"Mom, can we talk about this case I'm involved with?" Alex said. "The letter writer I told you about said a whole family by the name of Williams was murdered in their country home, and that the killer and bodies were never found. We've now discovered some new evidence, and the St. Catharines police have reopened the case." She paused. "The letter also said that this case somehow involves my own family, so I had to check that out. I discovered there was a woman by the name of Lila Stratsfield. I thought she might be a relative of ours. We were always close to Grandma and Grandpa Stratsfield, but I'm not sure about any cousins."

A frown appeared on her mother's face, but Jessica didn't saying anything.

Alex knew this wasn't going to easy, so she pressed on. "I figure you must know her. I wanted to talk to you before the police do. They'll be talking to relatives on both sides of the family." Alex hesitated. "Mom, I believe the letter writer wants this killer to pay for what he did."

Both of her parents looked at each other, then at her.

"Lila is my sister, and she married a man named Allen Williams," Jessica said. "I'm sure you remember your cousins, Anne and Rachel. They were about your age, but they lived in the country and we didn't see them much." She sighed, not wanting to tell her daughter about all the trouble they'd had. "They left town years ago with their family. It broke my heart. It was such a disappointment that I couldn't be part of their lives, but I've put it out of my mind over the years. I have no intention of getting into it again. Whatever you think you've found, I'm sure it has nothing to do with us."

Stanley, however, was only too aware of what was going on. "Alex, dear, I think sometimes things are not what they seem. Maybe this is better left alone. Nothing can be gained by stirring up old memories."

Ginny furrowed her forehead. There was something that Alex's parents weren't telling her. She looked from one to the other.

"It isn't that easy, Dad," Alex persisted. "I'm sure Chief Merritt in St. Catharines doesn't believe they just moved away, and neither do I." She stopped herself from telling her mother about the bodies in the cemetery. Lorne didn't want anyone to know about that. "Mom, they're going to find the person who wrote me that letter, and when they do, we'll finally know for sure what happened."

"I'm sorry, dear," Jessica said. "I don't know what to tell you."

"Mom, if you happen to think of anything that might help, call me. I'm sure the case will be wrapped up soon."

Jessica sat forward, about to get up. "Ginny, it was nice meeting you, and you're welcome anytime. Alex, please keep in touch, and drop by for dinner one evening. There's always room for a couple more at the table."

"Thank you," Alex said. "I'll do that."

Stanley got up from his seat and walked the girls to the front door. He even went outside with them.

"Please don't get into this with your mother," he said to Alex as they reached the Suburban. "It will upset her. You see, she was close to your Aunt Lila…" He lowered his voice. "Because you're not the police, I can say this: she believes Lila killed Allen and buried him somewhere out in the back forty and left the country with the kids. Allen was crazy in those days, brainwashing the kids against our family. Actually, he brainwashed them against his own too.

"Your mother decided last year to learn more about her ancestors. She thought I might want to help, being retired and all, so she sent me to the cemeteries around the area. I was in Canborough one day when decided to walk over that mound in the back. I saw these weird depressions in the earth that looked almost like graves, all in a row. As I got down to look more closely, my foot caught in some branches and I took a tumble. I panicked for a minute, thinking I'd broken something. When I stumbled back up, I discovered a cross made from a couple of branches. Someone had carefully constructed it from branches, and even tried to engrave something on it. Well, weather had taken its toll and worn away whatever had been there.

"I discovered there were seven graves. The first thing that came to my mind was Lila, Allen, and the rest of their missing family. To tell you the truth, I never believed they moved away. I had several theories, but that's all they were."

Stanley sighed. "Now you know who wrote you that letter. Alex, I was fed up with your mother driving to that boarded-up house every year. I suppose I could have gone to the police, and I should have, but I didn't want your mother to hurt anymore… and I knew you would look into it. My concern was for your mother. In fact, I'm still worried about her. I would rather she not know I wrote the letter until I feel it's time for her to know the whole story. I made you that ridiculous phone call, too, and I'm sorry if I scared you. I was afraid what the killer might do next. I can see that you have to find out who killed them, no matter what. I love you, Alex."

He kissed her forehead gently. "Ginny, we'll look forward to having you here again."

Alex just stared at him, shock, her mouth open, her breathing shallow. "Wow! Okay, Dad. I'll do my best, and you know something, I'm glad you did it. And I'm happy for the phone call." She smiled at him. "Chief Merritt is really very nice. You'll like him."

She kissed him on the cheek and walked to the passenger's door. She climbed into the Suburban as Ginny assumed the driver's seat.

"Let's go," Alex said, still surprised at her father's confession. "I need to get out of here."

She reached out to pet Spider as Ginny pulled out of the driveway and onto the street. She even gave him a couple of treats. He ate them happily.

"Let me know if you see a park," Alex said. "I'd like to take Spider for a run."

CHAPTER ELEVEN

NIAGARA-ON-THE-LAKE

Alex and Ginny stood at the front door of a lovely home later that afternoon, ringing the doorbell. The view of the lake was magnificent, and Niagara Falls itself was only a few miles further up the road from where Lorne lived.

Lorne opened the door, smiling widely. "I only arrived five minutes before you. Come on in. I'm so glad you didn't change your mind about staying here. You'll be a lot safer."

He reached down and rubbed the dog's ears. Spider didn't seem to mind at all.

"I have a great fenced-in back yard where you can run and chase bugs all afternoon if you want," Lorne said to the dog.

Spider gave him a bark of approval and Alex smiled.

"It's a humid day, but never mind, we have air conditioning." Lorne led them into the large hall. "I might as well get you settled in. Can I let Spider out? He'll be safe there, and he may need to go."

"That would be great," Alex said.

"I will be just a minute." True enough, he was back a minute later. "Alice, my housekeeper, will let him back in when he's ready."

Next, he led them up a magnificent old stairway built from rich walnut and shaped like a half-moon.

"I love living here on the lake," he said as they climbed. "I bought this house two years ago. The minute I saw it, I fell in love with it. I wanted to be a little way from work and this was the answer."

"So you've only been chief for a couple of years?" Alex asked, surprised.

"Three years, two months, and the days... well, who's counting?" They reached the top of the stairs where a hallway stretched out before them. "Here we are. I'm putting you in side-by-side rooms. I hope you like them. I hired an interior decorator when I moved in."

He had hired the interior decorator to make the place more comfortable for when his mother came to visit from Toronto. She complained that it was the only time she ever saw him, but he did try to make it home on long weekends.

Lorne opened the door at the end of the hallway. It was larger than Alex would have expected, painted light beige with accents of pale green. There was a small desk perfect for her laptop, and a couple of comfy chairs. A large television sat on a credenza across from the bed.

"Just put your bags in either room, this one or the one next door," Lorne said. "I'll wait for you downstairs."

Ginny decided to take the room next door. It was decorated the same, except that the accents were a rich yellow. Both rooms had small bathrooms, although their large mirrors made them look bigger than they were.

After they had settled in, they made their way back downstairs.

"You two seem to be getting quite cozy," Ginny said. "He seems like a nice guy."

"There's something different about him. I can't quite put my finger on it."

"Surely you don't think he's your killer?"

Alex almost laughed at the suggestion. "No, Ginny, you misunderstand. He's just different somehow from the other guys I've dated."

She definitely didn't think Lorne had anything to do with the murders, but if she was honest, she had considered that a different cop might have been involved. Maybe someone close to Judge Strandell, although she didn't want to tell anyone her suspicions yet.

They walked through the downstairs hall, admiring the glass doors that led into the living and dining rooms respectively. On the other side of the hall was a large kitchen and sitting room, with windows looking out the back of the house.

"I hope the rooms are satisfactory, ladies." Lorne gestured for them to join him in the sitting room. "Please sit down. Dinner will be about an hour from now. When it comes to cooking, Alice is the best. I love to eat, but can't boil water."

Spider ran in next, sniffing about and making himself at home.

"Don't worry about him," Lorne said. "I like dogs. Anyway, he's just looking around."

For the next half-hour, they chatted and engaged in small talk. Anyone listening would have heard hearty laughter and the cordial conversation of old friends.

Eventually an older woman with gray hair walked into the sitting room.

"Lunch is ready," she said, smiling at Lorne.

"Ladies, this is Alice. She's worth her weight in gold." He grinned at her. "Don't put on any more weight, Alice, or I won't be able to afford you!"

She giggled. "Oh, Chief. I would work for you for nothing."

Alice left the room, her funny little snicker following her.

"I know you'll enjoy her cooking," Lorne said, standing up.

Alex led the way because she had been closest to the door, even though she didn't quite know where she was going. Then she remembered that the dining room was through one of the glass doors off the hall.

"Please, just sit anywhere." Lorne took a seat at the pre-set table.

Alice brought in a salad of mixed greens with pine nuts and small slices of fresh strawberries. She had also prepared several different kinds of sandwiches, including egg, cucumber and cheese, and chicken. The homemade bread was delicious.

For dessert, they had scrumptious banana and strawberry pie with fresh fruit, covered in a bright red gel.

"Now that we're filled up, let's go and relax for a bit," Lorne suggested.

They did just that. The conversation turned to the region and how it had changed over the years. Lorne's mind kept drifting back to the case, though. It would be easy to find the killer if they could figure out his reason for killing the family.

"My mind is still on this case, no matter how I try to forget it," Lorne said during a lull in the conversation. "The more we delve into it, the more it looks like the oldest daughter is our killer."

"You think she killed her own family?" Ginny asked, surprised.

"She seems the logical one, with her boyfriend." He noticed the clock on the wall and stood up. "Sorry, I have to go back to work."

He knew that women loved to shop, so he gave them direction to a few nice stores in the area.

Alex and Ginny shopped for the rest of the afternoon, making up her minds to forget the Williams family and take a break. They had a delicious snack at a small restaurant and then headed back to Lorne's place, their shopping bags telling the story of a great day.

They only back a few minutes when Lorne returned. After dinner, they watched television and the late news together.

"I'm tired and ready for bed," Lorne said, yawning. "Ladies, I'm sure you will find the beds comfortable. I'll see you in the morning."

Alex got up from the couch and went to the door of the living room with Spider.

"Lorne, I'd like to take Spider for walk before I settle in for the night." She turned to Ginny and added, "I won't be long."

"It's late," Ginny said. "I'm not sure you should go alone."

"I won't be alone. I have Spider."

"I could use the walk too," Lorne said. "Do you mind if I come along?"

"That would be fine." Her gaze was ever so friendly.

They left the house, making their way to the side of the road. It was a gorgeous night. The moon glowed and the nearby river sparkled like glittering diamonds. Just across the river, the United States was a vision of millions of lights in the dark night. So close, but so far away.

"What a magnificent place," she marveled. "Lorne, you have it all. The perfect job, the perfect house, a fabulous Landrover, and probably the perfect girlfriend somewhere too."

He wanted to smile. "Umm… I'm not sure how to answer that. I had everything you just mentioned, including the perfect girlfriend back in Toronto. We were engaged, but I broke it off when I accepted the job here. Actually, it was more a mutual agreement. We thought we were in love, but knew there was something missing. They say girls are looking for a knight in shining armor. Well, I think guys really do look for someone like their mother, even if they would never admit it. You know how the old song goes: 'I want a girl just like the girl that married dear old Dad. She was the girl and the only girl…'"

"'Dad ever had,'" she finished.

They both laughed. Spider, not wanting to miss out, barked his two cents.

"As for the rest," Lorne said, taking in the beautiful view, "it may sound corny to you, but I have an awesome God who walks with me, every step I take. He has provided for me very well. I was saved several years ago, when a young girl was kidnapped in Toronto. I was a rookie cop and we couldn't find her. When we did, her mother's faith led me to a church where the door was open and I walked in. It was very small and nothing special. It didn't look like I had imagined a church should look like; I had expected statues and glitter, and I'm not sure what else. Anyway, I walked right up to the front and a man stood there in jeans and a plain T-shirt. He asked me if he could help me, and then he led me to the Lord. I've never looked back."

Alex wanted to jump for joy. *Lord, you've done it again. This is truly a miracle.*

Lorne turned to look into Alex's eyes. "I suppose you'll go find a hotel in St. Catharines now, away from this screwball who talks about a God you don't understand and don't want to know about. I never force my religion on anyone."

She wasn't sure what to say at first.

"You've put me on a spot," she said after a while, chuckling. "Lorne, we do have an awesome God. It will forever amaze me how he directs our paths, just like the Bible says. I'm a Christian myself, and I'm quite happy to stay with you."

After a brief hesitation, she went on to explain what her father had told her earlier that day, about having been the one to write the letter.

Soon they circled back and returned to the house. Alex went right upstairs, said her prayers, and thanked God for this man whom she was fairly sure she was falling in love with. Then she got into bed and fell asleep before she knew it.

Lorne didn't go right to sleep. After his prayers, he sat by the window. He liked Alex a lot. She was smart and interesting, although he might be too dull and boring for her. If this case took long enough, who knew what might happen? Could one fall in love in such a short time?

She was right. God did work in mysterious ways.

But it was unlikely she didn't already have someone special in her life. She was too beautiful to be alone.

Oh well, he thought. *Time will tell.*

He drifted off to sleep with her face in his mind.

CHAPTER TWELVE
THE RESTAURANT

The next morning came quickly. As she got ready, Alex had her time with the Lord, asking for his guidance for the day ahead. They had a great breakfast and then Ginny went outside to sunbathe and look after Spider while Lorne picked up Alex.

"Where are we off to today?" Alex eyes brightened, so happy to be with Lorne and all that was going on.

"I have to check out Keith Hanselford's relatives. They live not too far from the falls. I understand they have a bed-and-breakfast right on the main drag. It's my understanding that they've been there for years."

It took them forty-five minutes to arrive at the huge house on a corner lot. A colorful sign out front advertised the rooms for rent.

They climbed several steps to the veranda, which wrapped right around the front and the east side.

Her eyes went to the gorgeous trees and magnificent view.

"Lorne, so many of the houses have these amazing verandas."

"With a view of the escarpment, who could blame them?"

Lorne pressed the doorbell on the bright red wooden door. From inside, a melody greeted their ears, the tune somehow familiar.

The door opened and a young woman smiled at them.

"Welcome to Niagara Falls," she said. "Are you looking for a room? We have some lovely rooms, including a few special ones for newly married couples."

"Well, thank you," Lorne said brightly. "Unfortunately, we don't come under that category at the present time." He turned to Alex, amusement spreading across his face.

"I've tried, but the man just won't say yes," Alex said. "Maybe one of these day he'll give in."

His lips formed a puckered smile, then he took out his badge. "I'm Chief Lorne Merritt of the St. Catharines police. We're looking for Keith Hanselford, or close relatives of his."

"I'm his sister, Rebecca. Everyone calls me Becky." She paused a minute. "I haven't seen Keith since… let me see, I would have been twelve years old. Please come inside. I'll get us a coffee."

They followed her into a colorful sitting room. Sure enough, she wasn't long gone before returning with coffee.

"Keith was a rascal," she said. "He was so hyper and always getting into one thing or another. I knew he was up to something when I saw him take a bunch of food from my mother's pantry. I asked him what he was up to, but he just said it was a secret, and I promised not to tell anyone if he told me what it was. Well, he said that his friends Larry and Marshall were going on a holiday to Vancouver." Becky looked down at the carpet. "I knew Keith liked Larry a lot. My parents weren't happy about their friendship. I liked Larry too, although he was a little different. Keith thought our parents would be upset if he went along. And when they found out he had quit his job, my parents were furious. Anyway, he left town with his friends and never came back."

She went on to explain that her parents had hired a private detective after a few weeks, but they never found him.

"I tell you, he was my mother's favorite," Becky continued. "She kept saying, 'When he comes back, I'll kill him.' Of course she didn't mean it. She passed away last year… cancer. My father is in a nursing home and he has dementia. I blame Keith." She let out a long sigh. "I'm sorry, but that's all I can tell you. Do you mind my asking why you're looking for him now?"

Lorne gave her a short excuse, and then they left with a little more understanding than when they'd arrived.

* * *

Ginny sat at the kitchen table, finishing her cup of coffee. Phil had dropped in and was drinking coffee too.

"Ginny, what are you doing today?" Phil asked. "This is my day off."

"Not much. I was going to babysit Spider and just enjoy the sun."

"How about going for a ride? I can give you a tour of the area. I've lived here all my life, and it might be fun to see it through new eyes."

"Okay. Give me a few minutes to get ready."

She went upstairs to change into lightweight slacks and a light T-shirt. She also brought a sweater, just in case. She had been looking forward to sunbathing, but she told herself that it would probably be a bit boring to stay in all day.

Phil drove her to the falls and gave her a great tour. She had a wonderful time visiting places she had never been to, like the Rainbow Bridge that led to the States. The Horseshoe Falls alone were amazing. All that water and power was astonishing. She could feel the mist in the hot morning air. It felt wonderful on her skin.

Later, they had dinner in a lovely place along the shore of Lake Ontario. The day had been perfect.

They were just getting ready to leave when a young man walked up to their table.

"Excuse me, Detective Hudson, do you mind if I have a few minutes of your time? My name is Ted Fraser." Without waiting for an invitation, the man sat down. "I hear you've reopened the Williams case. I'm glad. I knew the Williams family rather well, and now that I'm older, I'd like to talk to someone about them. That is, if you're interested."

Phil was very interested, especially in learning something that Lorne might not know yet. Even Ginny could see what a great opportunity this was for him.

"Yes, of course," Phil said. "I'm interested in anything that might help us."

"I was seventeen, going on eighteen, when the family disappeared. I didn't say anything at the time, but they... well, the parents were rather weird. Our parents didn't want us hanging out with those kids."

The waitress appeared, bringing Mr. Fraser a coffee. He refilled Ginny's and Phil's cups.

"Unknown to my family, I dropped by the Williams farm earlier that awful day," Ted began. "I was sort of dating Rachel, who was sixteen at the time. But we dared not tell our parents. Rachel was very special to me. You know, it was first love. Puppy love maybe. Her father was very strict, though, and the girls weren't allowed to date. He said he was going to pick out their husbands. So we used to meet out behind the barn where no one could see us. Well, we were out back when her brother Joey came looking for her. He said they were having company and his dad wanted everyone to go inside, clean up, and prepare to meet the guest. The guest was bringing someone who was going to marry Anne, and Mr. Williams wanted everyone to be on their best behavior."

"This is what Joey told Rachel?" Phil asked.

"Yeah. Rachel was so upset because she knew Anne loved Marshall Wallberry. Anyway, Rachel told Joey that she would be along soon. She didn't know who this guest was, and she didn't think Anne knew either. Anne had been planning to run off with Marshall. She really loved him.

"Because Rachel didn't want her father to see me, she immediately headed for the house. I stayed a fair while, wondering if Rachel and I could run away someday too. At least I wouldn't have to worry until she reached the age of twenty. Detective, you have to understand that I was graduating high school and off to college in the fall. I was a little older than Rachel and had no plans to get married, but I didn't want to lose her either. Back then, farm kids married young and had no or little education like the city kids did. We were the first generation to be given the chance to become something besides farmers. But Mr. Williams had plans for all his girls.

"That was the last time I ever saw Rachel. I've tried a dozen times to determine just how long I stayed behind the barn before heading home. I was thinking about our conversation, our friendship, and time just got away from me. When I left, I had to hop a fence and walk across the old Miller farm. But before I could hop the fence, I heard two weird sounds. It could have been a car backfiring, and at first that's what I thought it was. I turned away and huddled down so nobody would see me, and I waited for a long time. Then, when I finally got up the nerve, I looked up—just in time to see Mr. Williams round the corner of the barn. He was in a big hurry and then, well… I've thought about this for years. I think I saw him drop something in the pigpen. I thought it was a gun, and… you know, as a kid, I got excited."

Phil listened with his mouth hanging open, surprised at what he was hearing.

"I waited until he was out of sight again," Ted continued. "Then I went into the pigpen to see if it really was a gun. The pen stunk like you wouldn't believe. It was downright awful. My folks didn't keep pigs, so I wasn't used to it. Well, I couldn't see any gun, so I decided to look in the barn. To this day, I will never forget what I saw. Two men were lying on the cement floor. They looked dead to me, shot in the chest.

"Then I heard some talking outside and knew I had to get out of there. I couldn't go back out the door, because that's where the voices were coming from, so I made for the ladder that went up into the hayloft. I lay down behind some bales, afraid someone would see me. That's when Mr. Williams came in with some men. I couldn't see them, but I heard their voices—"

"Excuse me," Phil interrupted. "How do you know one of the men was Mr. Williams if you couldn't see him?"

"To be honest, I don't know. I just thought I recognized his voice. The only thing I remember for sure is that one of them said, 'They're dead.' I'm sorry. The rest I'm not sure about. I know I heard a couple of trucks pull up, and they seemed to load up some of the animals. I heard a most awful racket as they pulled the huge pigs into the barn. I was never so scared in all my life.

"When I heard the barn door close, I climbed down and looked around. They had taken the smaller pigs and the livestock. I guess they couldn't get the biggest animals into the trucks, so they left them behind. Anyway, what could I do? I waited in the barn for a long time, terrified of being discovered. When I finally worked up the nerve, I snuck a peek out the door and flew around the back of the barn, away from everything. I headed for home as fast as my legs would take me.

"I have to be honest, Detective. I never told a soul. I was afraid. Maybe someone else would have done different, but I didn't want the old man to come back and kill me too. I still miss Rachel today. I would give anything to know what happened to her." Ted sighed, so glad to have finally gotten this off his chest. "Rachel didn't come to school for the next few days. I went back to our place behind the barn and waited, but no Rachel. I waited three days in a row. Then we heard that the family had moved away. I figured that whatever happened in the barn that day made the family move quickly."

Phil wanted to call Lorne right away, but he didn't. Maybe he was just trying to impress Ginny with his authority. It was exciting to know things that Lorne didn't.

Before leaving, Ted gave Phil his business card and agreed to talk again if he could be of any more help to the police. He then abruptly left the restaurant.

"Well, if that doesn't beat all," Phil said to Ginny. "That makes it sound like Mr. Williams is the killer. I'll let Lorne know. Ginny, I would love to look closer at that pigpen."

"So why not do it? You're a cop too." She thought a little ego burst would do him good.

His chin raised as he pulled his gut in. He seemed to stand a little taller.

They were about to leave when a woman walked up to the table and stopped them in their tracks.

"I'm sorry to bother you," the woman said. "Are you Chief Lorne Merritt?"

"No, I'm Detective Philip Hudson, ma'am."

"May I sit down a minute? I think that was Ted Fraser who just left your table." She sat down where Mr. Fraser had been sitting. "I won't take too much of your time. I'm Mabel Thornton. You know, there's not much that goes on around here that I don't know about. Everyone is talking about the police opening up the old Williams case. I expect that's why Ted was talking to you. He liked Rachel. We were all so young back then…"

"Anyway, I need to tell you something. We all knew Marshall was in love with Anne. We grew up going to the same school and came from neighboring farms. I often went over to the Williams house. I was always very welcome there, so I also got to know one of the older brothers, Gerald. I called him Jerry, and I liked him. But Rachel warned me that if the day came when I wanted to marry Jerry, I would have to come live on their farm for the rest of my life. According to Rachel, the girls in the family were going to be married off at twenty to wealthy men, and the boys would eventually run the farm.

"The farm was huge and doing well. I don't know how many acres, but it was a lot. Even so, Mr. Williams wanted to expand it and make it the most productive farm in the whole area. He figured that might happen with his sons running it.

"That very morning, Rachel told me that she'd overheard their father talking to their mother about me and said that one day I would make Gerald a suitable wife. Anyway, I didn't stay too long. As I was making my way back down the laneway, I saw Barbara hurry into the house, with Joey right after her. They seemed to be in a hurry.

"Don't ask me why, but I didn't go home. I guess I was curious about what was going on, so I tucked myself behind a bush and watched as a car drove onto the driveway and two men got out. Well, not really men. One was Marshall Wallberry and the other was Keith Hanselford. Marshall was seeing Anne, and that was no secret to anyone. We all knew her family disapproved and that there were lots of fights over this, but they still dated. Anyway, they left the car and made their way to the back entrance that led to the kitchen.

"I stayed right where I was. Now that I think about it, I was a nosy kid. Anyway, it must have been a good twenty minutes, maybe longer, before Marshall came out with Mr. Williams. The two of them went into the barn, and I had the good sense to stay hidden by the bushes. A little while later, I saw Mr. Williams come back out alone. I also noticed how dressed up he was, like in church clothes.

"Then the strangest thing happened. Jerry came out, got into Marshall's car, and drove it out into the field. I lost sight of it. Sometime later, Jerry came back, almost at a run. He was all dressed up too. It must have been another fifteen minutes before two more men arrived in front of the house driving a fancy car—sorry, I don't know what make it was, I wasn't interested in that sort of thing. Anyway, they got out and went into the house by the front door. They were all dressed up too.

"I watched for a while longer and nothing seemed to happen. Then I heard shots… well, it may not have been shots, but it scared the bejeebers out of me. I tell you, I was too afraid to move. I was like a frozen statue. To this day, I remember that my body wouldn't move. I stayed there, crouched like a scared rabbit in a hole.

"Then another couple of trucks pulled in. One of the men who'd gone inside came out the front door again and talked to the men in the trucks. After that, they drove somewhere to the back. A few minutes later, I heard the pigs squealing and complaining and men swearing. I thought they must be killing the pigs! I threw up all over myself, too afraid to move.

"Finally the trucks drove off and I ran away just as fast as my legs would take me. I never told anyone what happened, and besides, none of it seemed real to me. You know, Detective, sometimes I think it might have been a dream. Only I know now it wasn't. I put the dress I had been wearing into the garbage. never wanting to think about it again." Mabel paused, taking a deep breath. "I wanted you to know, if I can help in any way, call me. I'm a teacher at the Murphy Road Public School."

Without saying another word, Mabel got up and left. Both Ginny and Phil stared after her with puzzled expressions on their faces.

"Let's get out of here before someone else comes looking for you," Ginny said. "I've had enough of this."

In no time, Phil was dropping her off at Lorne's front door. They shared a goodnight kiss. In some ways, it surprised them both.

Ginny went inside and leaned against the closed door, wondering how it had happened. She had kissed him back, and that had been a really big mistake.

CHAPTER THIRTEEN

FINDING THE GUN

Alex got up and dressed. Another day was here and already the sun was shining warmly through the bedroom windows. She talked to the Lord and asked for his protection for Lorne and Phil in looking for the killer, and Ginny as well. She read several psalms, a couple of proverbs, and ended with Proverbs 16. It seemed to say something to her about her current problem. She read and reread it, and then these few verses were read again:

> *A man's heart plans his way, but the Lord directs his steps. Divination is on the lips of the king; his mouth must not transgress in judgment. Honest weights and scales are the Lord's; all the weights in the bag are His work… In the light of the king's face is life, and his favor is like a cloud of the latter rain. How much better to get wisdom than gold! And to get understanding is to be chosen rather than silver. The highway of the upright is to depart from evil; he who keeps his way preserves his soul.* [5]

She knew what she saw in a certain verses, but others didn't always see the same things. That was what she called the magic of

---
[5] Proverbs 15:9–11, 15–17.

the word. Every person was different, and what God had to say to them could be different too.

Finally, she prayed for the soul of the person who had killed the Williams family. She asked, if it be God's will, for him to lead them to the killer.

Alex walked down to the kitchen and found Lorne sitting at the table, already waiting for her. He didn't look happy.

No wonder, she thought. *He has so much on his mind, it's a wonder he can think at all.*

She noticed Spider was eating in the corner and couldn't have cared less that she had arrived. He had really taken to Lorne.

"Spider, I know you're eating your breakfast, but how about coming to see me?"

He totally ignored her. The moment he finished, however, he trotted over to her side. She bent down, cuddled him, and they talked a bit. Then he lay down beside her.

"Dare I ask what you have planned for today?" she asked Lorne as she joined him at the table.

"I have a list of people I want to see. When you went to see your parents, you talked to them about the case, right?"

The question worried her a little bit. "Yes, I did."

"Remember Kathy, the lady in the farmhouse you were talking to when you first arrived? She told you about a red truck. Well, she just called me and gave me a name to check out: Jessica Rutherford. Another name is Willow Webster. Apparently Lila and Willow were best friends."

Alex sighed, frustrated that her family was being pulled into this mess. "As you must know, Jessica Rutherford is my mom. Her sister Lila married into the Williams family. As for Willow, I don't know her." From his piercing gaze, it seemed to her that he thought she was keeping something from him.

"All right," Lorne said. "I'm going to see your mother. Do you want to come with me? You don't have to go, but I have a job to do. I don't want you to get upset with me, though."

"You know, Lorne, my mother isn't the easiest person to get along with. She still sees me as a kid. I don't think that will ever change."

"All parents go through that, to some extent." He briefly looked at the clock on the wall. "By the way, Ginny was up and out of here with Phil before breakfast. Something about checking on some gun. I didn't ask questions."

Alex knew that Ginny and Phil were getting chummy with each other, the eye contact and smiles between them a little too personal.

"As long as he keeps her busy and she's not bored, I'm fine with it," Alex commented.

Lorne had a lot to do and dared not admit to Alex that he liked spending time with her. They had only known each other a few days, but there was something special between them that was growing every day. He hoped this visit with her parents didn't change that. It was strictly business. As long as she remembered that, they should be all right.

* * *

Phil and Ginny drove up to the Williams farm in a black unmarked police cruiser. Police tape had been erected around the place, so Phil parked as close as he could without driving into the taped area.

"Let's go," Phil said to Ginny as they got out of the car. "I have to speak to one of our officers."

They ducked under the tape and approached the house. The door had been left wide open.

"Anyone here?" Phil called. "It's Detective Hudson."

Another detective appeared in the dim light. "What can I do for you?"

"Hi, Walt. We have a tip we want to investigate out back. I'll need to do some digging in that pigpen. We'll also need a couple of rakes and shovels. See if you can find any in the barn."

"Okay, but I don't think your shovels will do the job," Walt said. "I expect the ground is clay and near impossible to dig. Do you want me to call for a small earth-mover?"

"Good idea. By the way, this is Virginia."

Walt nodded to Ginny and smiled, then moved off to make the call.

"While we're waiting, Phil, why don't we go look for the car?" Ginny asked. "Mabel said it was out back somewhere."

"Okay." He shouted into the house, "We're going out back, Walt. Holler if you need me."

Walt stuck his head out from around a corner. "If he gets too hard to handle, Virginia, just call out and we'll come rescue you." He gave her a smile.

She chuckled. "Thanks. I'll remember that."

Together, Ginny and Phil walked to the back yard, beyond the barn. Their eyes scanned the tall long grass for miles. Other places, where birds had dropped seed, had grown wild wheat. Plowed corn husks lay rotting in the soil, left to rot.

"I wonder where we should start looking?" she asked.

"The ground would have to be fairly hard and level to drive a car out here. Let's try to the left of the barn, away from those huge trees."

They searched for a good forty-five minutes through all kinds of deep grass and bush before Ginny finally spotted something.

"Look over there!" she called. Something was hidden there, covered in vines and white flowers. "It might be a car. Kind of pretty, don't you think?"

All he saw was a huge lump of bush. With a bit of imagination, it could resemble anything.

"You could be right," he said after a while. "Whatever it is, it has to have been there a long time."

She nodded, thinking that if there was a car underneath, it might not be in bad shape. The vines may have protected it from the elements.

He shook his head. "I've seen some awful things in my time working in this department, but I'm glad I wasn't here when this went down. Quite frankly, I think it's a good thing Lorne reopened the case."

"I agree. No one should be allowed to get away with something that awful."

They moved quicker, excitement taking over as they came closer to the pile of vines. When they arrived, they couldn't believe their eyes. Behind the thick foliage, there was definitely an old car, the vines twisting through its open windows.

"Hey there!" a voice called.

Ginny turned and saw Walt and another man walking toward them.

"I was talking to Lorne on the phone and he said you're looking for a gun," Walt said when he reached them. He stopped and stared at the mass of flowers and vines, dismay written on his face. "Is that a car?"

"We think it's the car that belonged to the Wallberry kid." Phil's eyes traveled over the mass of foliage, shaking his head. "I had better call Lorne and tell him about this."

When he had the Lorne on the line, Phil told him where they were and what they had found. Lorne agreed to send over some technicians from the lab to check it out.

An hour later, three men arrived with enough equipment to excavate the car. Walt followed them to the car carrying a pair of heavy-duty cutters.

"Everyone, we have to be careful not to destroy any evidence," Phil instructed.

The whole group stepped closer, trying to figure out where to start. By now, word of their discovery had gotten out and several other officers had joined them, standing and talking, no one overly anxious to do anything.

One of the men did some cutting and pulled at the vine until he managed to get the back door open. Another started to help—but suddenly they all backed away, very quickly. Lo and behold, they'd discovered a family of skunks living on the floor of the car.

The next few minutes saw a great deal of activity as everyone vacated the area. The men all stood back, speculating about what to do next. Phil thought it was really quite funny.

The skunks may have been sleeping before, but now they were wide awake from the commotion. The mother came out first, staring at them. She climbed out of the partially open door and stopped on the ground by the front of the car.

"Looks to me like she can't make up her mind about who's going to get the first blast," said Walt, grinning.

"Can the little ones spray us?" someone else asked. "Maybe if we can get them out, she'll leave."

"Right," Phil said. "And how do you plan on doing that?"

"If you can get her sidetracked, we'll grab the babies and run for our lives. When she comes after us, we'll let them go."

There was lots of laughter and all kinds of suggestions, but no one ventured near the car.

"Look, everyone, I do know a little about skunks," Walt said. "I hear that they warn an attacker by stamping their feet... like that big one is doing now... and the aggressor better get out of the way. If you keep bugging them, they raise that big bushy tail. That's the warning signal that he's fully armed."

Phil took another look at the skunks. They looked a little bit like cats.

"The trouble is, guys, we need to get that car so these guys can do their job," Phil said. "We don't all day. I'll call the pest control and they can tranquilize them and take them somewhere else. You guys may want to go for a coffee and come back in about an hour."

Walt agreed. "A couple of us will stay behind and show the guys from pest control where they are."

Phil and Walt stuck around while the others dispersed. Then Walt found what appeared to be a safe spot under a large tree and sat down.

"I hope skunks don't climb trees," Walt said. "If they come my way, I'm running!"

Once pest control had everything under control, the men started to work on the car. They found the keys and all the ownership papers in the glove compartment, practically as good as new. The owner had been Marshall Wallberry.

By now, the earth-mover had arrived in the back yard. Its operator waited for Phil to tell him where he wanted the ground dug up.

"This was a pigpen many years ago, though it's all dried up now," Phil said to the operator. "I need you to take out about a quarter of a shovel load. Then put it to the side and we'll rake through it. We're looking for a gun, an important piece of evidence."

After some time of moving the earth and raking through it, Ginny realized how glad she was that Alex had lent her these rubber boots.

Phil starting to feel disappointed as another couple of detectives joined the work. At last, the third scoop produced the gun. The officers present cheered as though someone had just hit a homerun in baseball.

Phil placed the gun in a plastic evidence bag, still disappointed as the earth-mover filled the holes back in. It would take more than a miracle to get any prints off this gun. It had been working its way into the ground for too many years.

CHAPTER FOURTEEN

MEETING ALEX'S PARENTS

L orne and Alex pulled up to her parents' home.

"I know you don't want to do this," Lorne said. "You don't have to come in, you know."

Even if Alex hadn't come, he would still have had to interview them. Actually, now that he had met Alex he would have wanted to meet them anyway. Just not under these circumstances.

"I wish you had let me call ahead and warn them that we were coming," she said.

"I don't think it would have made any difference. Your mom doesn't know he wrote the letter."

"Please don't tell her. There will be plenty of time for that later, after we've solved the case."

"Just let me do the talking. They cannot blame you for this."

Alex frowned sadly. "You make it sound so simple, but they'll know I had something to do with it. My mother isn't an easy person to deal with."

"You just leave her to me. I'll give her all my charm. She won't be able to resist me." He grinned impishly at her.

They stood on the porch and rang the doorbell. A minute later, her father opened the door.

"Well, my goodness, this is a surprise. Two days in a row! Come in, my dear." Stanley gave a quick look to the stranger with her, figuring it was a cop.

"Dad, this is Lorne Merritt, the chief of police in St. Catharines. He's here on business, and he's been kind enough to let me go about with him on the Williams case."

"I'm pleased to meet you, sir." Lorne showed her father his badge. "Alex has mentioned you and your wife to me."

"When something this dreadful happens in a family, nobody ever gets over it completely," Stanley said. "Especially when there's so much confusion around it. My wife hoped it was over. We regret if our silence may have resulted in the murderer getting away." He led the way inside. "Please, come in and sit down, Chief. Just call me Stan. Everyone else does."

They walked through the hall to the kitchen.

"Your mother is out in the back yard," Stanley said to his daughter. "It's lovely out today. Would you like to go out? It's quite comfortable on the porch."

"That would be just fine," Lorne answered.

Stanley knew his daughter well enough to know that she didn't want to be here, so there must be trouble. His wife had never thought this case would ever resurface again—and if Stanley had just minded his own business, it probably wouldn't have. But every year on the anniversary, Jess went to that house and came away disappointed. He sighed. She thought none of them knew about her hopes that one day her sister would return with the rest of the family, all grown up.

He led Lorne onto a large, screened-in porch while Alex got them something to drink. Lorne appreciated how grand the porch was. He also noticed an attractive older woman in the yard. He realized how much Alex looked like her.

"Jessie, we have company," Stanley called. "Will you join us?"

Jessica walked toward the porch and appraised this young man accompanying her husband. She somehow knew this was going to bring up a lot of heartbreak.

"Dear, this is Chief Lorne Merritt of the St. Catharines Police." Stanley indicated his wife. "Chief, my wife, Jessica Rutherford. Alexandria's here too. She's in the kitchen."

"Our Alexandria!" Jessica said as she climbed the stairs onto the porch. "I'm pleased to meet you, Chief. Please sit down. What can we do for you other than to strangle whoever wrote that letter to my daughter? We thought we had put that terrible tragedy behind us, and now you're about to drag it all up again."

Lorne looked sideways at Stanley, remembering that Alex had asked him not to say anything. It was up to Stanley to tell his wife the truth. "I'm fairly new to the area and would have loved if this hadn't been dropped into my lap, believe me." He paused. "I also have to say, you have a very nice daughter."

"Thank you." Jessica sat in a chair quite near the young man. She wasn't looking forward to this, and she wished Alex hadn't come along. "Now, what can I do for you, Chief Merritt?"

"First, I want to point out that your daughter isn't responsible for me coming to see you. I have the names of several other relatives and friends, and I'll be going to talk to them all."

Jessica leaned back in her chair, staring off into the distance, somewhere beyond the screened porch. She felt herself being tossed in so many different directions. Did she want the truth to come out? The trouble was, she did and she didn't. She wasn't sure what to tell him. It was all so complicated, nothing but trouble.

"What can you tell me about the Williams family?" Lorne asked.

She wanted to say nothing. Did she want the truth to come out? The trouble was, she did and she didn't. It had happened so long ago.

Her eyes went to the young man. "My sister Lila was married to Allen Williams, but I'm sure you know that." She decided to tell Lorne the basic details and let him find out the rest for himself. "Lila was a schoolteacher until she married and retired to raise her children. Allen didn't want a working wife, although she ended up working just as hard as anyone, what with raising her kids, washing clothes, making meals, helping in the fields… the list goes on. I have to admit, I'm glad I was never a farmer's wife."

Jessica shifted in the chair to get more comfortable. She surveyed the garden beyond the porch.

"Chief, life isn't always what it looks like," she continued. "You know the saying that the grass is always greener on the other side? When you get to the other side, it's anything but. In a way, that was how I saw the Williams family. I thought my sister was happy, but she wasn't. And Allen was very good at reading people, but there was something about Lila he couldn't put his finger on, and it worried him.

"Years ago, I got a promotion at the bank. I was extremely busy, so I didn't see Lila as much as I used to. I went to the baby showers, of course, and I always saw them in church. Back in those days, we would have Sunday dinner together at my parents' place with Lila and the children. I didn't see anything wrong, and she never said anything to me about problems in her marriage.

"It must have been fifteen years into the marriage before we started to hear nasty things about Allen. She once told me that her husband didn't agree with girls going to university. He wanted to see that they had wealthy farmer husbands. Lila seemed happy with this. I tried to reason with her, but she wouldn't listen."

Lorne could see Jessica was struggling with every word she said.

"We saw less and less of her and the children. Whenever we invited them, Lila was too busy. One day I parked down the road from their house and waited until Allen left. Then I drove in and rang the doorbell. I called out to her several times, but she didn't answer. It was almost as if I could hear breathing on the other side of the door. Of course I must have imagined that. No matter what I did, the door never opened. I even threatened to call the police."

As she spoke, Stanley felt her pain. All he wanted was to give her closure and peace. He wished he had never written that letter.

"Then I did a very bad thing," Jessica said. "I waited outside the school where Rachel, Barbara, and Joey attended. Lo and behold, before I could even get to them, Allen arrived to pick them up. Next, I found out that Allen took out restraining orders against members of our family, so we weren't allowed on their land. I went to the teacher and the principal, and they denied me any right to talk to them, by their father's orders."

Jessica seemed about to continue, but Lorne put up a hand to interrupt. He needed to bring her to another part of the story, a part of the story he thought was more important to the investigation.

"If I can interrupt here for a minute," Lorne said, "what did you think when you learned they had gone missing? There's a lot of mystery as to what happened."

Again, that faraway look came back. "I waited until the police vacated the scene, since we still had an injunction against stepping on the property. One morning, my brother and I went to see the farm. It was locked up tight and the police had boarded up most of the windows. We couldn't get into the house." She paused and looked straight into Lorne's eyes. "I learned yesterday that you found the bodies. How many bodies were there in those graves?"

"There were seven," Lorne said. "We're not sure yet whose bodies we have, but we believe there were more people at the farmhouse when the murders happened. We have to account for everyone who was there."

Jessica looked toward the door to the house. A tear slipped down her cheek as Alex walked outside with glasses of iced tea.

"To be perfectly honest with you, I've wondered if my sister killed them," Jessica said. "But then I remind myself that she would never have killed her children, no matter how bad things got. Unless she thought she was saving them from Allen? There was obviously something very wrong in that family. It's easy to put the blame on Allen."

How can any of these people understand what I'm feeling? Jessica thought. *I thought found out that my sister is dead for sure and never coming back. How can I face it?*

"I was sure Lila would contact me sooner or later," she added. "I hoped they were alive somewhere. Now that I know they're gone, I want to see that justice is served. I'm not sure what justice looks like, in this case, but I guess that will depend on who you find and why they did it. Maybe you should find whoever wrote that letter. If it was someone from my family, I think they would have told the rest of us before now, where those bodies were buried, to give us some peace of mind."

"My dear," Stanley spoke up quietly, "whoever wrote that letter just found out about the bodies recently.

Alex couldn't help but notice that her father had a deep frown on his face. She knew he was doing what he believed was best for her mother.

Stanley's eyes shifted to watch Alex and Lorne. He liked this young man, and he had a good job. Yes, quite suitable.

"I can see my daughter has become a friend of yours," Jessica said, picking up on the vibe. "I should warn you, she has a mind of her own. She loves her job. And no matter how dangerous sit gets, she'll be right in the middle of it. I tell you, we never get over worrying about her. That's something the right man in her life will have to learn to accept."

"Okay, Mom, enough." Alex chuckled. She knew her mother didn't understand her views and walk with the Lord. "We're just good friends. You'll scare the poor guy off."

Stanley smiled at his daughter and winked. "We're very proud of her."

"Thank you both," Alex said. "You know I love you. As you know, I have holidays coming and I'll be here. We'll have plenty of fun."

Lorne smiled at them all, his eyes meeting Alex's. "Umm... does that fun include me? After all, we're neighbors."

"Well now, I'll have to think about that."

For a few moments, their eye contact said more than words. She was liking this man so very much.

CHAPTER FIFTEEN

MORE SURPRISES

When Lorne asked Phil to check out Willow Webster, the detective set off right away. Since he'd been taking Ginny just about everywhere lately, he decided to ask her to join him. She was hyped up to go after helping to find the gun.

They soon arrived at a house in the country. Neither of them had made any conversation during the drive, both lost in thought.

"This is nice," Ginny said as they looked at the home. "It's old-fashioned, but also modern in a way."

They left the vehicle and headed toward the house. It had a wooden veranda and gorgeous gingerbread trim. Phil reached out and rang the doorbell. They heard the sound reverberate through the house.

A man opened the door, staring at them.

"Are you the police?" he asked.

"Yes, sir, I'm Detective Philip Hudson, and this is Virginia Adams." He showed the man his badge. "Were you expecting us?"

"We knew it was only a matter of time before you showed up. Come in. My wife will make you a cup of coffee." They followed him inside. "In days past, we served tea in fancy china cups. Now it's good strong coffee in mugs. Time changes everything."

"True enough," Phil said. "We're looking for Willow Webster."

"That would be my wife." As he said it, they entered a huge, very modern kitchen.

Willow met them in the middle of the room. She wore jeans and a fashionable pink T-shirt.

"I'll put the coffee on," Willow said.

They sat down at the shiny oak table. A vase of fresh flowers stood in the middle. They immediately caught its sweet perfume.

"You know, no one came to see me after Lila and her family left town and moved," Willow said. "None of us wanted to admit having anything to do with Allen. It was kind of hard on us. Allen was my husband's brother."

She saw their eyes perk up, frowns appearing on their faces at the same time.

"I'm Justin Williams," the man said. "Good to meet you."

"Oh, I imagine you'll be in for many surprises," Willow added. "Let me tell you something: there was nothing wrong with the Williams family. Allen and Justin were both handsome and good catches. Their parents were well off by the standards of those days—not rich, you understand." She smiled, memories coming back to her. "When Lila and I started dating the Williams brothers, it wasn't the easiest courtship. The four of us double-dated as much as we could, and of course we both fell in love. But Lila's family disapproved, bigtime. Allen wasn't good enough for the Stratsfields. You have to understand, the Stratsfields and Rutherfords were high society."

"You know, falling in love was the most natural thing that could happen," Justin said. "Lila really loved Allen, so after they graduated he went to her father and asked if he could marry her. He had money for a down-payment to buy land and a nice house in the country. He also had a degree in agriculture and great plans for the future. Well, they did marry—against her father's wishes." Justin shook his head sadly. "Their relationship was good to start with. I never saw two people so much in love, and when things started to go wrong, about ten or so years later, I blamed it on the Stratsfields. They thought they were better than anyone back in those days. I hear they still do. Never mind, that's another matter. Mind you, it may not hurt to check into their family. Who knows? Lila had a weird sister by the name of Jessica who didn't like me either."

Willow brought he coffee to the table and sat down. "I'm not sure what went wrong," she said. "Lila wouldn't tell me, but when she needed to talk to someone, she called me with one ring and hung up so Allen wouldn't know. I have to be honest with you. I wasn't sure who was crazier, Lila or Allen." She looked at her husband. "You didn't know either."

"That's true," Justin said, grinning. "I still prefer to think it was her."

"Anyway," Willow continued, "I went to see her whenever it was possible. She became very agitated when Allen set up a marriage between some bigshot judge's son and her eldest daughter, Anne. She told me that Anne loved Marshall Wallberry. I had known the Wallberrys for years and they were a nice family, but Allen was insisting that Anne marry… let's see if I can remember the name—"

"I believe it was Larry," Justin interrupted. "Larry Strandell."

"Yes, that was it. Allen insisted they were going to get married quietly in a small church here in the country. Judge Strandell was going to see that Larry joined the same law firm his two sons worked at, so Anne would be the wife of a prominent lawyer. Well, Lila thought the boy was very strange. I didn't get what she meant, and Anne didn't love him. He creeped her out, Lila said. I remember that distinctly. I was beginning to think I was the only sane one.

"Then I got that single ring one day and ignored it—and not for the first time, I'm sorry to say. I was just too busy. Finally I made the trip to the apple tree where we always met. She was beside herself. All she talked about was that Anne and Marshall were going to run away together and she was terrified of what Allen would do."

"Excuse me a minute," Phil said, breaking in. He turned to Justin. "What was your relationship like with your brother? Were you not talking?"

"I wish I had a better answer for you," Justin replied. "I guess the trouble started a little later than Willow said, about fifteen years after they were married. It was quite sudden. I'm not sure exactly when we all stopped seeing each other at family get-togethers, but everyone was talking about Allen going crazy. And the more we tried to find out what was going on, the more he turned away from us."

Willow gave her husband a look of disgust. "Oh Justin, how many times did you go and knock at their door and they didn't answer even though you knew they were home? And he refused to discuss anything about the family when you did talk."

"That's true," Justin said. "Allen would meet me in town and we would have lunches together. He seemed fine to me, though. I just figured they had troubles as a couple, but they would work them out."

"He did that all right," said Willow. "He killed them all."

"Now, Willow baby, we don't know that." Justin looked to Lorne. "To this day, I blame Lila. And my wife blames Allen."

"Can you tell me about the time leading up to the disappearance?" Phil asked.

"My brother stopped talking to me and everyone we knew," Justin said. "I actually asked my parents if there were any mental problems in the family and they said absolutely not. They blamed it all on the Stratsfields."

Willow picked up the story. "Lila called me early one morning with her single ring, and I met her at the apple tree. She was walking in circles like a crazy lady. I got her to sit down on the ground with me and tell me what was wrong. She said that Judge Strandell was at their house and that he and Allen had made the final arrangements for the wedding, which would take place at the end of the month. The judge was a big man in the community, so they had to be very careful. He wanted his son married real badly. He was even going to give them a house in the Niagara area as a wedding present.

"Lila was going to help Anne and Marshall Wallberry run away after dark on the following Thursday. They were making plans to get married Friday morning, then head out west to Vancouver. I was a little worried. I even asked Lila if she might run with them... and then I was worried about what would happen to the children left behind. Lila told me that once Anne and Marshall escaped, Allen could do nothing about it.

"Then she really threw me for a loop. She told me that Larry was running away from home too, that he hated his father and didn't want to get married either. But Larry was so afraid of his dad that the poor boy started to sneak clothes and food from the house and leave them in the Williams' barn.

"Anyway, Marshall and Anne and Larry had made their plans, and Lila told me that she had her own plans and that I didn't need to worry about her. I asked her what she meant. I remember so clearly the look of sheer happiness on her face. I hadn't seen her like that in years. It haunts me to this day. 'I have it all worked out,' she said. 'Don't worry about me. Everything is going to change and everyone is going to be all right.'

"The next time I heard from her was Thursday, the day when the kids were planning to run away. I met her at the apple tree. It was raining cats and dogs, but I went anyway. Well, talk about excitement! Lila had new clothes made for all the children and they were going to attend Marshall and Anne's wedding on Friday morning. I guess Allen thought the cloths were for Anne's and Larry's wedding. Well, I was shocked, but she was on cloud nine. She said that she had come to say goodbye and thank me for being such a great friend. Her plan, I found out, was to take the children and leave Allen. I asked where she was going, but she said it was a secret." Willow looked down at her coffee cup, still full in front of her. "That was the last time I ever saw Lila."

Justin nodded. "Willow insisted that I go over and try knocking on the door Friday afternoon to make sure my brother was all right. She thought he was alone there and that everyone had left him. Of course, he didn't answer. I tried phoning and no one answered the phone either. Then, two weeks later, we heard the family had moved away, taking everything with them. Willow and I both went over and decided we were going inside no matter what. We didn't know what to expect and thought he could be drinking himself to death, or dear knows what else. We found the house boarded up tight. We walked to the back yard and saw that the fence was down around the pigpen. For the first time in my life, I knew fear. We left right then and went home. I called the police and asked them to check out the farmhouse.

"A policeman came to see me after and explained that they'd checked and verified with the schools that the kids had moved, taking transfers to schools out west. To be honest, none of us know what happened. I never heard from my brother again, and that's the truth. We figured that Marshall and Anne were living out west with the family, and that my brother had taken off to find them."

"Well, if it'll make you feel any better," Phil said, "I can tell you that none of that happened. After further investigating the farmhouse, we can confirm that several murders took place there."

Justin sighed. "That's what we feared. In fact, we've heard that you might have found the bodies. Is that true? News travels fast in small places like this."

Phil nodded and told them about the seven shallow graves discovered in the Canborough cemetery. When he was finished, he indicated Ginny.

"I haven't introduced you to Virginia yet," Phil said. "She's a newspaper photographer from Oakville. A reporter at her newspaper received a letter from someone who told her where the bodies were buried. The person didn't sign their name. Both of the girls are working on the story with us."

Justin filled their mugs with more hot coffee.

"Nice to meet you," Willow said.

Justin smiled and nodded. "You must have an interesting life."

"It certainly has been this trip," Ginny replied.

"I don't suppose you have any idea who wrote that letter?" Phil looked from one to the other.

Willow looked surprised. "No, of course not. I would have felt better knowing about those graves. I've lived with the most horrific pictures in my mind all these years." Her expression turned to confusion. "So the police have Allen's remains as well as the rest of the family? Does that mean we can give them a proper burial?"

"Well, we haven't identified the bodies yet," Phil said. "I'll see that you get word when we do. It could take months before we have the answers. I know that sounds like a long time, but we're working as fast as we can."

Phil stood up, and Ginny did the same.

"I can't thank you enough for all the help you've given us," Phil told them. "It's often the people connected to murder victims who give us the most help solving the crime. Anyway, we'll get out of your way." He took out his card and placed it on the table. "Call me if you think of anything else."

Ginny followed him out of the house. As they got into the police cruiser, Phil almost felt as though he had come from the crime scene.

"Well, you have to admit, you have lots of suspects to choose from now, even in poor Alex's family," Ginny said. "She's smart, though. Don't be surprised if by now she's figured out who wrote that letter."

"You may be right." He smiled, reached over, and kissed her. "You're amazing do you know that."

He had no doubt in his mind that he was in trouble. He had fallen in love, and that was ridiculous. He hardly knew her and he didn't care. Ginny's eyes seemed to peer into his soul, and he liked the strange feeling it gave him.

Who falls in love so quickly, and especially in these circumstances? Phil asked himself. *Only an idiot, that's who.*

"I think we should call it a day," he said. "I want to drop by the station and make sure everything's all right. Then will you let me take you out to dinner? Or do you want a home-cooked meal?"

"Whatever you want is all right with me."

They headed back to the police station and parked in the lot.

"You might as well come in," he said, getting out of the car. "You can relax inside for a few minutes. I won't be long."

"You know what? I'm going sit right here. Please, take your time. Just leave me your keys so I can listen to the radio if I get bored."

Once he was gone, she lay her head against the headrest and closed her eyes. There was so much to think about. She couldn't believe that she was working a crime case with Alex, and one so demanding and exciting. She wouldn't want to go back to the women's page after this experience. All she had to do was talk to James about transferring her to the crime section.

In no time, the door opened and Phil climbed back into the vehicle.

"I thought I might find you asleep," he said.

"No, I was just thinking." She told him how Alex had convinced her to take on this story with her, and then explained about her previous marriage and divorce.

In turn, he gave her a rundown on his life.

"I know it's too soon for you to get married again, or even consider it," Phil finally said, "but I'm not going to let you go, Ginny. Oakville isn't that far away. Come on. Let's go and get a nice supper."

* * *

Alex and Lorne were having dinner at his house when the phone rang.

"It's Phil. Excuse me for disturbing you," Phil said on the other end of the line.

"I hope the interview went well," Lorne said. Phil was a good detective, soon to get a promotion to deputy chief.

As Phil filled him in on what Willow had said, Lorne listened and realized they were getting closer and closer to the killer.

"I have some news for you," Lorne said to Alex after the call ended. "Ginny and Phil had an interesting day."

He explained what Phil had told him.

"You're kidding!" Alex said. "Maybe we'll make a crime photographer out of Ginny yet."

She was still amazed at how God always managed to put her in places she didn't expect. Even when things looked hopeless, God could see tomorrow. Ginny was a perfect example. Her friend had been so unhappy just a few days ago, but now she seemed to be turning her life around.

"Life is interesting, isn't it?" he said, smiling at her as though sensing her thoughts. "Do you know Psalm 37? It's one of my favorites. I love these verses, and I learned them by heart when I was a kid:

"Trust in the Lord, and do good; dwell in the land, and feed on His faithfulness. Delight yourself also in the Lord, and He shall give you the desires of your heart. Commit your way to the Lord, Trust also in Him, and He shall bring it to pass."[6]

"I like that one too, especially when it's put to music," she said, soaking in the verses.

"I believe God has a time for everything," Lorne continued. "I believe he is helping Ginny to regain her trust in him, and her hope for the future. I'm sorry life has thrown a curve at her. God really is amazing."

She nodded, agreeing that Lorne was absolutely right. "To me, it's even more amazing that you turned out to be a Christian and that we can be friends and work together on something as important as this case is. It has to be the work of God."

"Alex, if you're honest with yourself, can you say we're just friends?" Lorne asked. "I have fallen in love with you, and I'm fairly sure you have the same feelings toward me. I would have been the first to say that love at first sight is hogwash, but then I met you. Something has happened between us."

She nodded, knowing that he was right. "What scares me is the fact that we've known each other such a short time. I guess I feel like it's not real. Maybe it's the place, or that we're working so closely together. I've never worked with another person like we are."

"Well, we're not done yet." He stood up and gently pulled her out of the chair by the table, taking her in his arms.

They exchanged a kiss. It was something neither of them would forget for a long time to come.

---

[6] Psalm 37:3–5.

CHAPTER SIXTEEN
THE NEED TO KNOW

Two figures, both about the same height, scanned the cemetery. One of them, a young man, had short curly blond hair and round blue eyes. He wore jeans, a pale blue T-shirt, and a jean jacket slung over one shoulder. The other, a young woman, was a little bit shorter and her hair hung in ringlets on her shoulders. She too boasted bright blue eyes. She wore jeans, fit more tightly and showing her nice hips, and a yellow T-shirt with beading. A matching buttoned jacket was draped over one arm.

They had arrived in St. Catharines two weeks ago, a few days before the anniversary of their family's deaths. They had both needed time to get used to the idea of visiting this cemetery, and later, the house they had grown up in. It had taken a lot of courage to come back, and they needed to act slowly and carefully. They had always known the time would come to weigh the past and put everything behind them. They had to see justice done and clear their names.

They had driven by the homes of some of their relatives, and the houses looked just as they had remembered them. They hadn't been allowed to see their family members for so many years, which they had accepted at the time. But that was then and this was now.

They shed no tears and felt no guilt or regret. They felt nothing.

"Come on," the woman said. "Let's get this over with."

The man drove their car into the cemetery as far as they could go. They sat in the car, not wanting to get out but knowing they had to. First one door opened, then the other. They climbed from the car and started to walk. It was strange to be back after all this time, and they knew exactly where they were going.

They came to a place where the ground sloped down towards the back and the bush beyond. They stopped for a minute, immediately noticing that something was wrong. The sun had burned the grass in the rest of the cemetery to a crisp yellow, but not here. Freshly mown sod covered the area at the bottom of the hill. Their feet stood on lush grass.

"What do you make of this?" the young woman asked.

"I don't know. Maybe they're getting ready to bury more people here."

"It doesn't look like that to me. I can't even see where we buried them." She looked puzzled. "They must have found them."

"The grass is still fresh. It can't have been that long ago."

"It had to be the police," she said. "Don't you think?"

"Yes. How strange! Just when we're planning to come back, to put away the ghosts of the past? Maybe the sod doesn't mean anything. Maybe it's a coincidence."

"I don't think so. Look at this!" The young woman tugged on something bright yellow on the ground. She pulled up what appeared to be a piece of police tape. She then tucked it back where she had found it.

They stood in silence for few minutes, looking around them to make sure no one was around. With the knoll in the earth, they could only see so far.

"We knew it wasn't going to be easy," he said.

Just for a second, a face flashed before her eyes. A face from deep in her memory. She had thought she loved Marshall, but now she wasn't sure. It was so long ago.

"I wonder how long they've known."

"By the look of the grass, maybe a few weeks." He imagined his ma's face and a tear slid over his cheek. He had only been a kid back then. "What will they do with them now? They need to—"

"It's only bones," the young woman interrupted. "Their souls are in the hands of God."

"I know that, but they still have to be properly buried."

"Don't worry. We'll see that they are somehow. I hope we haven't made a mistake coming back here," she said. "If the police are involved, we could be in a lot of trouble. It may seem like a lifetime to us, but it's only been fifteen years."

She moved a few steps closer to where she knew her mother had been buried. A tear trickled down her face. The memories could bear so much sadness at times.

"We did nothing wrong," she said. "Always remember that."

She walked over the sod and stopped along the edge, close to the fence. She bent down and picked up a handful of sticks that seemed to have been raked under the grass. Then she walked to a nearby tree and broke off a couple of branches. She smiled at the young man as he did the same. They sat down on the grass like a couple of kids.

In the next half-hour, they had fashioned seven crosses and placed them in a line three feet apart from each other. They stood back and looked at each other, tears slipping from their eyes. They hadn't forgotten that tragedy of so long ago.

With the back of their hands, they wiped away their silent tears. There was no time for that now.

"Are you going to be all right?" the man asked. There was such suffering and sorrow behind his eyes.

"Just let's get out of here. I am terrified someone will see us." She spared another glance at the crosses. "You know, he's not going to get away with what he did."

"You frighten me when you talk like that. I couldn't live if anything happened to you."

"God has taken care of us ever since the day we left. Now he's going to settle some scores long overdue. God meant for us to come back, and here we are."

The man put his arm around her shoulders. "Remember Abraham. He didn't waver at God's promise, but was strengthened into faith, giving glory to God. I've hung onto the words of the Bible for so many years. God's word will see us through, just like it has all these years."

"Yes, I know," she said. "We wouldn't have gone to that church so long ago if we hadn't left home."

"We owe them bigtime," he agreed. "Let's get out of here and go see the house."

They climbed into the small car with an out-of-province license plate. The key slipped into the ignition and it purred like a cat. They made their way from the cemetery.

It took them a while to find the house, and when they finally drove onto the property they discovered a problem. Bright yellow police tape was very much in evidence. They quickly backed down the lane, not wanting to be seen.

They parked along the road.

"I can't imagine what has happened here after all this time," the young woman said, shock in her voice. "Surely they found everything when they investigated the crime all those years ago. How is it possible that they just found it now?"

She could still see the red blood soaking into the carpet, Larry holding Ma's hand... she would never forget that. Poor Larry must have been terrified.

"Yeah. And our family and friends from school had to have missed us." He looked at her with a frown. "Unless he figured some way to explain it all away."

"How could he? A whole family dead, and no one did anything until now? That's not possible."

He nodded in agreement. "We have to go in there, to chase away the bogeymen of the past. We have to ignore the police tape and make sure no one is—"

They were interrupted by a passing red truck.

"Excuse me," the male driver called to them through his open window. "You cannot park here. There's a police investigation going on at that farm. The police come by every once in a while and boot everyone off the road."

The young man rolled down the window and thought he recognized the driver of the truck.

"Oh," the young man said. "We'll move along. Thanks."

The woman put her hand on the side of the young man's face, acting as though they were just two lovers looking for a quiet spot to park.

The young man turned the key in the ignition and they moved past the truck. Neither of them spoke again until they were a safe distance away.

"That was close," the woman said. "What do you make of that? I'm fairly sure that was a member of Ma's family. I think his name is Ken. He hasn't changed all that much."

"Did he recognize you?"

"I doubt it. I look quite different now." She smiled at him. "No one would recognize you either, so tall and handsome."

He looked in the rearview mirror as the truck disappeared down the road.

"We'll have to figure out another way into that house if the police are watching," she said. "I think we may have to wait until dusk."

* * *

Further down the road, the man in the red truck pulled over and dialed a number on his cellphone.

"Hi," a woman answered. "Where are you?"

"I'm sitting on the side of the road that goes to the Williams house. There was a car here with two people in it. They're young, and you won't believe it, but I think the one of them for sure is a Williams kid. The other, I'm not sure."

"So the anniversary has brought them back. I had lost all hope. Ken, was one of them Lila? I have to know."

"I don't think so. But I couldn't get a good enough look to know for sure." He paused. "I would know those Stratsfield eyes anywhere. And I'll tell you something else. The driver was a man with large blue eyes and curly blond hair. Jessie, it had to be Joey." His words exploded with excitement.

"That's not possible. It just isn't!"

"Yes, Jess, I'm sure. I wanted to tell him who I was and ask him all kinds of questions, but I didn't."

"That's good," she said. "Do you think he recognized you? We don't want to scare him off."

"I'm positive he didn't. He was so young back then."

"Not as young as all that if he killed his whole family." Some bitterness came through with those words. "Ken, who could do such a thing? His mother, father, brother, and sisters... it's so awful. I just can't believe it. You're sure the other one wasn't Lila?"

"She wasn't old enough, but I may be wrong."

"All right," she said. "What are you going to do now?"

"I'll follow them to find out where they're staying." Ken paused. "I'll call you later, and then pick you up."

"Okay. Just don't let them see you."

With that, he ended the call.

* * *

A second truck had also been keeping a look out on the farm. The two men in the truck had been watching the property ever since the police had reopened the case.

"He was right," one of them said. "This isn't good. Wouldn't you have thought they would have enough sense to stay put wherever they were?"

"Yeah, he'll have no choice but kill them now."

"You don't think he would try to implicate us, do you?"

"Nah. He'll figure a way out of this, believe me. He knows what he's doing."

"Well, I have to call him." The man put his phone to his ear and made the call. When someone answered, he said, "You were right. They are here, and they're staying at a hotel in St. Catharines."

"Okay, stay with them," the voice over the phone said. "They could put me in jail for the rest of my life. I want to know what they're up to. If I have to get rid of them, I will. I don't want any loose ends. They should have stayed wherever they were."

* * *

Inside the hotel room, the two young people sat at the table watching television.

"I wonder if all the stuff we left behind is rotted away," the young man said between forkfuls. "I guess my room will look exactly the same." He pictured in his mind the toy cars and trucks he hadn't wanted to leave behind, the teddy bears he had loved so much.

"The place should be covered in dust and cobwebs." She didn't want to remember too much. It just brought back so much pain in her heart.

"I don't think I can go into Ma and Pa's room."

She laughed out loud. "Imagine if our friends today heard us refer to our parents as Ma and Pa? What a joke that would be."

"Yeah. We're not farm kids anymore, yet they're still Ma and Pa." He stopped eating potato chips from the bag for a moment. "Well, not anymore. You know what I mean."

She nodded and ate another chip from the bag in her hand. "I keep thinking about that guy in the red truck. You sure he didn't recognize us?"

"Yes, I am. Ken is one of our cousins, but he was out of bounds to us when we were kids, and he probably still is. He's a Stratsfield, and we aren't. We'll never be good enough for that side of the family. Pa made that clear." Just thinking about it made him angry. "It's not fair. We've done really well, considering everything. No one would blame us for what we did."

She shook head, remembering the fear inside her. "Do you really believe that? Of course they will. They'll never understand the decision I made that day. We've paid the price every day since, and I'm always looking over my shoulder, wondering if he found us."

"I still wonder what would have happened if we had stayed."

"That's easy. We'd be dead too. No way would he have left us to tell what happened. You know that as well as I do. And the law would never understand, not in a million years."

He agreed. "We have a plan and we're going to stick right to it. And when it's finished, we'll go home. Home. We're not staying here. This will never be home again, and that's that. Remember, you agreed."

"We're not going to make the same mistakes Ma did," she said. "And you're not going to replace Pa. You're better than he ever was. Remember what that therapist said? We don't carry baggage. We're Christians too, and that makes a difference."

He laughed. "Wow. Look at the Stratsfield coming through in you."

"Maybe." She remembered her ma's gentle eyes, so penetrating, the slant of her head, and the few happy moments they had shared. She had been a Stratsfield.

They continued talking and making plans as they finished their snacks. When they had decided what to do, they went out to the car and started it. Before they could leave the lot, however, the same red truck from before pulled in behind them and a woman got out. She walked to the driver's side window and knocked on it.

The boy opened it halfway.

"Do you remember me?" the woman said.

"No," he said. "Should I? I'm just visiting from out of province. Maybe you're mistaking me for someone else." He smiled at her. "It must be nice to live so close to Niagara Falls."

"I was hoping you might remember me, Joey, although we saw very little of you once your father went ballistic. Sorry, I shouldn't have said that. I'm your Aunt Jessica and this is your Uncle Kenneth, my brother."

I go by Joseph now, the man thought, but he didn't say anything. For the first time, he noticed Ken standing behind her.

"We've waited so long to find out what happened all those years ago, and obviously you have the answers." Jessica realized she didn't sound very friendly, but she didn't care. This boy had killed Lila and the rest of his family.

"Look, I have no idea what you're talking about. We are simply visiting from out of town. You've made some mistake."

"Oh, I don't think so," Jessica said. "I always hoped one of you would come back someday. I just didn't know who it would be. I have missed my sister so much. I've lived for the day when the truth would come out." She pointed across the parking lot, where a police cruiser waited. "That's my daughter Alexandria, along with the chief of police and another detective. They're going to arrest you for murder."

Joseph gasped, as did his sister.

"Well, so much for doing what we thought was right," the woman said, her eyes bearing dark, cold anger. "You're a Stratsfield. What more could we expect?"

"Yes, a Stratsfield. A name your father poisoned in your minds," Jessica said. She paused, looking more closely at the woman. Suddenly, she realized who she looking at. Anne! She had no idea what to think. Astonishment filled her gaze.

"We didn't kill anyone!" Joseph said.

Jessica nodded. "Okay. And where better to hear your story than in the family home?" Despite her shock, her voice remained angry. "The chief will follow."

Joseph looked at his sister. She had given up so much for him, and now he had to stay strong for her. He liked to think he was the man in family.

The truth, however, was that she was the strong one and always had been.

"Let's get it over with," Anne said. Her voice was strong and held a note of rebellion and apprehension. "You have no right to judge us for what we did."

The three vehicles left the parking lot, followed by two unmarked police cruisers.

"We have money if we need a lawyer," Anne said to Joseph as they drove. "Just keep remembering, we haven't done anything wrong. They might be able to charge us with leaving the scene of a crime, but that's all."

"How can they? We were fleeing for our lives!"

Anne looked out the window at the passing fields. "We're going to be all right. Let me do the talking, at first anyway."

* * *

In the police cruiser, not much had been said. Finally, it was Lorne who broke the silence.

"Are you all right with your mother being in on this?" he asked.

"Yes," Alex told him. "Without her, we never would have found Joseph or Anne. I tell you, I never would have guessed those two were still alive. They'll have some story to tell."

"Do you think Anne killed her own family?" Lorne asked.

"I have to tell you, Lorne, I had it figured all wrong. I'm usually good at figuring out mysteries, but not this time. Anyway, I don't think it could have been Joey. He was too young to do something like that."

"It wouldn't be the first time a child killed his parents. But in this case, I doubt it. The girl had more of a reason. Anyway, we'll soon hear what really happened." Lorne looked at her, concern written on his face. "You're sure you're going to be all right?"

"Yes, but I don't think my mother is. I suspect she'll get them the best lawyer money can buy, even if it turns out Anne did it. The abuse in that family must have been vicious." She hesitated. "How would you know what you'd do unless you lived through something like that?"

Lorne didn't want to think about it, and fortunately he didn't have to. They had arrived at the farmhouse and pulled into the laneway.

Saved by the bell, he thought.

* * *

In the darkness, the two men keeping an eye on the farmhouse watched the arrival of police cruisers. They sat in their truck, wondering what to do.

The driver picked up the phone, keeping one hand on the steering wheel. He stole a quick look at the man beside him.

"Real trouble, boss," he said. "There's a whole parade of cop vehicles here now, including the two kids I told you about. They just turned into the lane. I don't think we can do anything at this point. Do you have any suggestions?"

The man on the other end of the phone didn't answer. Sitting in his den, he leaned back, tipping his chair a little. A great sigh escaped his throat as he hung up the phone.

He sat back up, his mind miles away. Then he bent over and opened the bottom drawer of his solid mahogany desk. He reached far to the back and took out a small box and a brass key.

This den had been his sanctuary. He'd spent a good many hours here making plans.

He stood up and walked to a wall cabinet that had been especially built for his expensive gun collection. He opened the door and stood staring at its contents. At last, he carefully took one out from where it had been lying. He held it for a few minutes like it was a precious item.

Next, he returned to the desk and opened the small box with the key. He reached inside and removed two bullets. When he was done, he locked the box again and returned it to the back of the drawer. He laid his precious item on top of the desk's blotter surface, the two bullets beside it.

He sat for a minute, just looking at it. It took up all his attention. Then he looked toward the window and staring out beyond the curtains, seeing nothing. All he could think about was what must be going on at the Williams farmhouse.

He stood again with another key in his hand and made his way to a marvelous piece of cabinetry, also on the wall. This cupboard had gorgeous glass doors, and behind them all sorts of bottles. Some of them were worth a fortune.

He unlocked it, reached in, and took out the rarest and most expensive of them all. He smiled as he locked the cabinet again and walked out the room with the bottle in his hand.

"Are you all right, dear?" a voice called.

"Yes, I'm fine."

He made his way to the dining room, heading straight to the large walnut buffet. He took out a gorgeous, long-stem crystal goblet and then made his way back to his den. He laid the goblet on top of the desk and sat down, looking from the gun to the empty glass.

A downcast expression was written all over his face. His eyes, filled with fear, stared into nothingness. He then lifted the gun and inserted the two bullets.

Standing up, he headed for the back sunroom where his wife was curled up in a comfy chair reading a book. He walked up to her with one hand behind his back.

"My dear, I have something for you."

She looked up at him and smiled. "For me?"

"Yes, my dear, but you must close your eyes or it won't be a surprise."

She laughed and did as he said, expecting something with diamonds, like a pin or a necklace.

He raised the gun. It only took one shot.

The man turned away, not wanting to see her die or the wide, staring eyes of death.

He left the room, taking his time, and walked back to his den. There was no way she could have handled being alone and carrying the burden of what he had done. To know the truth about Larry would be more than she could stand. She had never realized what a disappointment Larry had been to him.

He sat back down and got as comfortable as possible in the chair. His eyes drifted to the empty glass. He picked up the bottle, and in moments he had filled the glass three-quarters full. He set the bottle back down and held the glass. Then he looked at the gun lying on the desktop. He'd had no idea it was going to be so difficult to put it to his head and blow his brains out. He took several sips. He had killed before, so what was the big deal?

There was no other way out of this mess. Why had those two come back?

He sighed, shaking his head. A judge couldn't go to prison. If that girl hadn't been such a fool, they all could have lived happily ever after.

He finished the glass of courage, though it didn't seem to be much help. He filled it again, and bit by bit the bottle emptied.

Finally, he stood up and paced around the room. He wasn't quite as steady as he should have been. He looked toward the window, came back, and sat down again.

* * *

The cavalcade of vehicles pulled up in front of the Williams farmhouse. Jessica and Ken left their truck and joined the police. Together, they approached the car holding Anne and Joseph. The young people got out of their car slowly, Anne taking hold of her brother's hand. They both stared at the house.

"Please, just give us a couple of seconds before we go in there," Anne said in a begging tone. "We're not going anywhere. Just give us a little space."

Anne and Joseph stepped back a few feet. Everyone else watched them, not sure what to expect.

"It looks awful, doesn't it?" Joseph said, his eyes fixed on the house. "It has no paint. It looks depressing. It reminds me of the old places we passed that day in the truck. I'll never forget."

"Well, it's better not to think about it." She wondered where all the white paint had gone. Even the paint around the windows had peeled off, and someone had boarded some of the windows.

"Do you believe in ghosts?" Joseph asked her.

"That's silly. You know we have God on our side. He'll see us through this. Remember, there's a time for everything. God has given us fifteen years to heal, and now we must do what's right." Anne turned to the expectant group. "We're ready to go in."

She could see the anticipation on every face as they started to walk—not to the front door, which they had never used, but to the back door.

Joseph handed Lorne the key.

"The door is already unlocked," Lorne said, handing it back to him.

No one noticed the tear slip down Anne's face as Joseph put his hand to the knob. The door opened and he went right in, slowly, Anne squeezed his hand for support and Joseph, too, tightened his grip. He needed it as badly as she did.

They stood staring at the small space, remembering hanging their coats here when it was cold outside. They had always taken off their shoes or boots in this room.

They carried on into the kitchen. It looked almost as it had the day they'd left. Anne remembered having been so afraid some of those men might come back. Even now, a sudden nocuous feeling invaded her mind.

"Would you let us look around?" Anne asked, addressing Lorne. "We'd like to see it one last time."

"Are you sure? Don't you want to get it over with?" Lorne looked at both of the young people, then nodded, gesturing for them to go. He turned to Alex. "It has been fifteen years. What are a few more minutes?"

Nonetheless, he instructed Phil and another officer to stay right with them.

Anne and Joseph started by looking around the kitchen, still walking hand in hand.

"Do you mind if we go upstairs?" she asked.

Lorne nodded. He could only imagine how hard this must be for them, killers or not. He actually felt sorry for them.

They went up the stairs next. Neither of them spoke a word.

They stopped in front of the wide open door to their parents' bedroom.

"They're not here!" Joseph exclaimed in a childlike voice when he saw that the room was empty, as if he had expected to see their bodies. "Poor Ma and Pa."

When Anne came to her old bedroom, she entered alone. Joseph and Phil watched from the door as she ran her hand over her former possessions with loving care.

Next, Joseph went into his old room at the end of the hall. Tears fell slowly, and he let them fall. The wallpaper with teddy bears made him smile. The room looked just the same. He opened the dresser drawers; the clothes were just as he had left them. He lifted an undershirt, so small. He turned back to Anne, standing in the doorway.

"I think you have grown some," she said, smiling at him. "I'm sorry we left so much behind, but you know we had to."

He nodded in agreement. He looked at all his childhood toys, long forgotten as he had grown up. He'd had so much, yet they had been such an unhappy family at the end. He wondered what would have happened if Anne had married that creep Larry. Would everything have been all right? Would the family still be alive? A lot would have changed by now.

Anne watched the expressions flit across Joseph's face. She knew her brother so well. She had been his sister, and then a mother to him.

"Joseph." She spoke his name sharply. "Don't go there. Pa was abusive to us all, and to Ma. There's no room for what-ifs."

She turned and walked back into her old room. She reached under the bed, causing Phil to make a defensive move.

"It's all right," she said. "I just wanted to see if my suitcase was still here. I was going to take it with me when Marshall and I left. It was full of special clothes, but I just couldn't take it after what had happened to Marshall." A touch of anger showed on her face,

She shoved the suitcase back under the bed. That was another time, and this was now.

She looked at the bedspread her mother had made, all by hand. It had taken weeks to finish and was a thing of beauty. She wanted to keep it, if it wasn't rotten. It would be something to remember her wonderful mother by.

She walked back out with such a sad expression on her face. She was close to tears, choosing not to go inside any of the other bedrooms.

"I'm sorry," Joseph said to her in the hallway. "You're right. Even if we had stayed, nothing would have changed."

They walked back down the stairs to meet the others in the kitchen.

"Remember, I'll do the talking," she said to him.

Anne glared at Phil, who had overheard their words upstairs, then moved on with Joseph to the sunroom. This room hadn't changed either. The only thing different were the red-brown bloodstains.

Phil was almost in tears himself as he watched these two. Their faces revealed so much emotion, so much sadness, hurt, and pain.

Jessica kept back, watching the drama unfold. Even Stanley wouldn't be able to understand what this meant to her.

CHAPTER SEVENTEEN

WHAT REALLY HAPPENED

Everyone pulled out chairs and sat at the large kitchen table. Some of the police officers stood nearby. The room was filled with emotion. Terrible stories about this family had long circulated among them. Some felt sorry for Anne and Joseph; others thought they had gotten away with murder far too long.

Anne rather looked around the table. Their coming back hadn't been what she had expected, what it should have been.

"I have to start with Larry Strandell," she began, "which must seem like a strange place to start. We knew Larry was different, and you know, even today it's not accepted by all people. First of all, his father was very much against any kind of homosexual persuasion. I'm sure if you were gay and came up before him in his courtroom, so sad too bad, you're done. Both Marshall and I knew he was gay and we felt sorry for him. His father was being very mean, constantly saying it was nonsense and that all he needed was a good woman. He simply refused to believe his son was gay. He had made many dates with young woman, expecting Larry to ask any one of them to marry him. Of course he didn't. He got to the point that he just kept telling his father, 'One of these days, the right girl will come along.' He promised he would get married when that happened. That gave him time to do some planning."

Anne looked at Lorne, a question in her eyes and the slant of her chin.

"I have no idea how Pa knew the judge," she continued. "We, Marshall and I, only knew what Larry told us about him. One day the judge came to see Pa, surprising us all. We all had to have a peek at Larry's father, even Joey." She chuckled. "This was a really big deal. I well remember Pa asking us to come in and meet the judge, and he introduced us all."

The stillness in the room was haunting as Anne looked off to the kitchen window for a minute, streaked with dust marks.

"Then Pa told us to go and play, like we were small children, which was ridiculous. But to me, he said, 'Sit down, Anne, and join us for a few minutes.' I will always remember those few minutes for ever. The judge looked at me, and his eyes seemed to get larger and bore right into me. I was so uncomfortable. He said, 'You're a beautiful young girl.' When he used the word 'girl,' I knew I didn't like him one bit. He asked me how old I was. I stared right back, hoping he could see how much I hated him. Just for a minute, I was afraid of him. He was like my pa, mean and nasty. I stood up and told him I was twenty. Then I left the room, almost daring Pa to call me back. He didn't. I'm not sure what I would have done if he had. I have to tell you, Pa had seemed to go kind of crazy in those days. Ma blamed it on the homemade whisky he got from old man Lindsay's still.

"Later that night, Pa called me into the parlor and told me he had chosen a husband for me. He said I was going to marry Larry, that he would make me a great husband and that the judge was going to buy us a house and set Larry up in a firm. I would be rich and well cared for."

Joseph put his head down, feeling an ache in his stomach for Anne. He had been so young and hadn't understood any of this at the time.

"I tried to explain that I loved Marshall and we were going to get married, but Pa started to throw things around the room, toppling a couple of chairs, swearing at me, calling me dreadful names. I was sure he was going to kill me. I was terrified and finally agreed. Ma tried to reason with him and received a black eye, a sprained arm, and almost a broken hip. Well, I couldn't wait to tell Marshall. We immediately made plans to run away and get married, unknown to Pa. We were going to head as far west as we could go." Anne smiled suddenly. "I'll tell you something funny. When Marshall's friend Keith heard of our plans, he decided to go with us. Larry wanted to come too. To make a long story short, Ma helped us and we did get married.

"We were originally going to leave on Thursday and get married Friday morning, but we needed more time and changed our plans so that we would leave on the weekend instead. Ma wasn't worried. She figured that if Pa found out about it, he would be angry but wouldn't be able to do anything about it.

"Well, on Friday night, before we were ready to run, Pa came home in a happy mood. The judge and he had made arrangements for Larry and me to get married right away. Ma was to put on a feast of food for the judge and his wife and the rest of us as a celebration. She felt she had no other choice than to tell him that I had already gotten married.

"What surprised me more than anything was that he was calm as you can imagine. He told me to call Marshall and bring him home so that we could celebrate our marriage. We should have known something wasn't right, but I was so happy that Pa was going to accept our marriage. I just didn't think. I did as he said, telling Marshall that everything was all right. An hour later, Marshall and Keith arrived. Pa greeted them like old friends. I was amazed as how nice he was. He even wanted to give us some of his cows and pigs for a wedding present. So Marshall and he went out to the barn. I wasn't interested at all. Keith just followed the noise and excitement into the sunroom to play games with my siblings. Well, sometime later, Ma and I heard what sounded like gunshots. I didn't know what they were up to, and for a minute I almost convinced myself they had gone out to shoot some tin cans or something, to prove who was the better shot. I looked at Ma and she just shook her head, shrugging her shoulders like she had no idea what they were up to. I decided to find out."

A couple of tears rolled over Anne's cheeks.

"Excuse me," she said, wiping her eyes on the shirttail of her top. "I ran to the barn and stopped at the open door, never expecting what I was looking at. There stood Pa with a gun in his hand and he looked up and saw me staring at him. He walked right by me and said, 'Say goodbye to your lover and get dressed for your wedding. As a widow, you are free to marry again.' And he walked away, just like that. It took me a few minutes to realize what he had done. All I remember is throwing myself on top of Marshall and crying and trying to somehow bring him back to life. Ma came and pulled me off his body and made me walk back to the house."

Alex and Jessica didn't look at each other as they brushed away tears. Even some of the police officers wiped their eyes. Some of the people listening shook their heads others took great breaths. Loud sighs echoed in the room.

"I remember Ma saying, 'Never mind. We'll find a way out of this, but for now go along with him. Put on that white summer dress.' I was like a statue, not caring, not feeling, as I did what she said. Pa had ordered the whole family to hurry and get dressed because there was going to be a wedding.

"To tell you the truth, after the shock of seeing Marshall's body, I blocked out as much of it as I could. I remember Ma washing the blood from me. I followed her around in a daze, feeling numb.

I found the other kids in the sunroom, all dressed up but playing their games and having fun. Keith was trying to beat them." She looked at Joseph, smiling at him as they relived this last positive memory. "Then Ma said, 'Joey, come here.' She made him get into the cupboard along the wall of the sunroom. She warned him that Pa was going to get into one of his rages and he was stay in there until she told him to come out. Joey was the youngest and Ma's baby. She knew Keith could take care of himself, and the rest could take a beating if necessary. Besides, they wouldn't fit in the cupboard." She paused and looked around the table. "Would you like me to show you where it is?

Lorne nodded. "Yes, that would be fine."

Anne stood up and led them into the sunroom. One of the walls was covered in cupboards. There were drawers and lots of doors, each a good size. Anne showed them a cupboard on the bottom row, near to the window. She opened it and looked inside, then bent down with a look of surprise.

"I guess you couldn't get in there now," she said to Joseph.

He smiled at her. "I bet I could if had to."

"Ma told me to hide in the back of her bedroom closet and pull all the clothes tightly in front of me and stay there," Anne said. "I didn't want to. I was afraid for her, yet I didn't want to marry Larry. So I did what she told me to do. But I'm a little inquisitive, so I made my way to the top of the stairs and listened. I heard the front doorbell ring. Then I recognized the judge's voice, and in no time I heard the arguing. The voices became louder and louder—and then I heard shots. I froze right where I was standing. I pictured Marshall on the barn floor and tears fell in a downpour. I headed for the closet, more because I didn't want anyone seeing me crying. I felt like I was never going to stop.

"I can't tell you how long I stayed there, crouched as far back as I could get. I really don't know. It might have been an hour or more. I had seen so much and the man I loved was dead. I couldn't even think straight. Then, for some reason, I felt peace like I had never known before. I now believe it was God. But suddenly my mind cleared and I realized that a lot of time had gone by. I stood, stretching as best I could in the crowded closet, and carefully opened the door. I walked out of the room very slowly, listening for any sound. I stood again at the top of the stairs for some time. I was afraid to go down."

Joseph stepped forward, cutting in. "I heard the gunshots and I knew what they were," he said. "I was scared, like a little rabbit running for his hole. I was used to hiding and not moving in case Pa ever found me. I didn't know who was shooting at who, or at what. I didn't even know about what had happened in the barn. But a few minutes later, I heard four more shots, right outside my hiding place. I burrowed deeper into the cupboard, if that was possible."

Anne jumped back into the story. "I made my way down the stairs one a time, going slow and making sure no one would hear me. I had no idea what I would find, certainly nothing like I did. When I came to the bottom, the house was so quiet. I thought maybe they had gone out somewhere. I walked into the kitchen, not sure what I was thinking."

She paused, suddenly remembering the food on the stove and the tall wooden chairs sitting empty. She remembered the bright-flowered cushions sitting on each chair. The tablecloth had matched. Her ma had spent hours sewing to make it all look so smart.

She blinked and carried on speaking. "I could still here the noise from the computer game in the sunroom, but I didn't dream that anything was wrong. I didn't notice the lack of yelling and hollering, the sounds of everyone having fun. So I walked into the sunroom." The colors of red and brown flashed before her eyes. "I can't tell what was going through my mind. I just can't remember. At some point I realized Gerald, Rachel, Keith, and Barbara had been shot and were dead. I do remember looking at them, and wondering where Joey was."

Her mind took her back in time, searching for her little brother, seeing Rachel's dead eyes as if they were turned to look at her, her mouth open as if in surprise, seeing the hole in her head and the blood on her clothes. Barbara had fallen on the floor, also covered in blood. She remembered grabbing her stomach. Gerald and Keith also had head wounds. They were a gruesome sight. She had gagged, but no food came up. Her stomach almost heaved again from the clarity of the memory.

"Sorry," she said quietly. "I was lost in thought for a minute. I wanted to get out of there as fast as I could, but I had no idea where. Suddenly, like a miracle, I remembered that Ma had put Joey in the cupboard. I said, 'Joey, it's me, Anne. Are you in there?'"

"I will always remember Anne's voice," Joseph said. "I opened the door and climbed out. I don't know why, but when I stood up and looked around, I was surprised to see that Barbara and Rachel had tumbled off their chairs onto the floor. I have no idea why that surprised me. It really didn't register in my mind that they were all dead. I just stood there, truthfully, trying to figure why they were on the floor. Then Anne grabbed me up, trying to keep me from looking at them. She pulled me from the room. My legs didn't want to move when I realized what had happened."

"He was giving me trouble," Anne said. "I knew it was shock. I slapped him hard and he started to cry. I was really mean to him. I told him to stop it at once, and I knew that I sounded just like Pa. I knew we would be next if the killer was still around. Whoever it was had shown no mercy, so we had to run away. I couldn't coddle or baby Joey. Our lives could were at stake." She paused, with a dazed look in her eyes. "I've gone over those few minutes over a million times in my memory. I realized much later that time was passing strangely. It all happened faster than I thought."

"She did eventually tell me she was sorry for slapping me so hard," Joseph said with a grin.

Anne looked at him with all the love and care that a sister has for her brother. "I had to make him see the danger we were in. I'm very proud of how we handled ourselves. We've overcome a lot in our lifetime.

"After that, I grabbed his hand and we left the sunroom. I had to know what had happened in the parlor. We went hand in hand. I told Joey to stand at the doorway and not to move as I walked into the room. I saw Pa, and he was dead. What surprised me most was that Larry was holding Ma's hand, and they had dropped dead right where they stood. I honestly didn't know what to do. All I knew was that our lives were very much in danger.

"Suddenly, I heard this awful racket. I returned to the doorway and held on to Joey to make sure he didn't do something I couldn't fix. We walked to the kitchen, and then over to the window. I thought the sound was coming from the barn. So help me, it was the strangest sight I had ever seen. Three men were loading animals from the barn into the back of two small trucks, and the cows were objecting. They were putting the chickens into a big create. It really was a tug of war for them to finally close the back of the trucks.

"We couldn't figure out what was going on. I thought someone was stealing the cows, but there was nothing I could do about it and I didn't dare show myself. There were more animals than could fit in the trucks, so I figured they would take the first load and come back for the rest. Then another small truck came flying by, dust flying in the air. I was even more surprised as I watched one of the men cut the fence to the pigpen with huge cutters. They loaded the small and medium pigs into the truck that had just come. The pigs were even more stubborn. They went in eventually, and then the men closed the tailgate.

"I'll never forget the next hour as long as I live. Someone opened the barn doors wide and all the men tried to force the biggest hogs inside. In spite of all our misery, both Joey and I laughed. It really was funny. Those hogs were so strong, we figured the men would end up in the barn while the hogs drove away in the trucks. Sorry, that's really stupid."

Lorne could just see in his mind all that pink flesh mingled with arms and legs pushing and pulling, men toppling about, and it was hard to tell who was who among the huge pigs. He caught Phil looking at him and grinned.

"When they did finally get the pigs inside, they closed the barn doors. The men got in the trucks and they drove back toward the house. I quickly grabbed Joey, telling him to follow me back upstairs. We hid in Ma's bedroom closet again, burying ourselves as far back as we could. We were so scared I was shaking, holding on to Joey. We never made a peep, and neither of us moved.

"We waited to hear the trucks leave before abandoning our hiding place and making for the kitchen. I made Joey sit at the table while I thought about what to do next. I decided there was no way Pa was going to be blamed for another man's murders. Pa was dead, and he hadn't killed Ma, Larry, Keith, and the others. So it was my idea to take the bodies out of the house. I have no idea what made me think of that. I looked all around me, and the first thought I had was our old, beaten-up truck. Pa only used it for transporting garbage to the dump. The kids used to do wheelies and all kinds of things with her, and he never minded. We had even driven tractors to plough the field in perfectly straight lines, so we weren't strangers to driving. It was always parked out behind the barn.

"But then I remembered the good truck, the one Gerald had taken to the co-op to get feed for the chickens and cows. He always parked the truck at the back where it was easy to unload stuff. I grabbed Joey and we practically ran to the barn. The whole way there, I was somehow praying for God to help us, even though I didn't know God yet. I don't think I had ever done that before."

She looked up at Lorne and smiled at him. But then her face went white as snow.

"Then I remembered Marshall, Larry, and Keith, and they deserved to be buried too. The animals were stick making a racket in the barn, so I carefully tried opening the door. I dared not let them out. Joey helped me, but I didn't want him to see inside the barn. I had no idea how I was going to get Marshall out. Once I managed to get the door open a few inches, all I could see were the dogs…"

She stopped talking and started to cry buckets of tears. She couldn't help herself.

No one moved at first, but then Joey and Jessica rushed to her at the same time to help. Jessica lifted her gently and held her a few minutes until she stopped crying.

"Thank you," Anne said. She blew her nose on a couple of tissues that someone had put in her hand. "I had to leave them behind. But at least the truck was there. I'm sure if any of those men had seen it, they would have taken it. We should have just gotten out of there right away, but instead we went to the shed out back and got Pa's big wheelbarrow. I was very careful, listening for any unusual noise, ready to hide again if necessary. Joey helped me and we loaded the bodies with lots of old tarps into Pa's truck. They were all so heavy. It was a wonder we both didn't break any bones.

"I have no idea why we weren't both crying, we just weren't. Shock, I guess." Anne sniffed and wiped her nose again. "When the bodies were loaded, I sent Joey to the shed to get some more garbage bags and a couple of shovels. When I actually say it, my stomach wants to heave my breakfast."

She closed her eyes for a minute, then looked up at the woman sitting next to the police chief. She looked so much like her mother, who had held her lovingly when she had cried. This woman had the same eyes and hair and was about the same size too, only older. There was even something in her face that reminded her of Ma.

"I remembered a cemetery where Ma had said our relatives were buried. I looked on a map and found where it was. That was the first time we took a moment to see ourselves—we were a mess and had blood on us. So we went back into the house to get clean clothes, and it was then that I decided we needed to run away. If the judge knew we were alive, we would be dead too. He was crazy and a killer.

"We had to bring as many provisions as we could. I filled some pillowcases with food that I knew would keep, and I made sure we took all the peanut butter Ma had to spare. There were five jars, I remember even now. Then Joey helped me fill a bunch of Ma's canning jars with water. We took anything I thought we could use that wouldn't be missed. I remember taking three loafs of fresh baked bread. Once we had everything loaded in the back seat and on the floor of the truck, I covered it so it wouldn't be noticeable. Then I covered the bodies. We put two huge tarps over them and fastened them down with big stones from the yard. I had to make sure they didn't blow off while we were traveling to the cemetery.

"Joey was so quiet, and I was miles away in thought, concentrating on the road and the traffic. I had driven sometimes into the nearest towns to get groceries, but never on the highways. I hated the huge rigs." Anne sighed. "May I have a glass of water please?"

She took a quick glance at the people around her, really glad to be getting this off her chest after all this time.

"After we left the cemetery, I decided that I wanted one last look at our house, so I drove back. Just as I was about to turn into our laneway, I heard hammering. The pounding sure sounded like more than one hammer. I didn't go any farther. I went back down the lane, but we were leaving and never coming back."

CHAPTER EIGHTEEN

THE TRIP WEST

"I'm curious how you ended up getting out west," Jessica asked, bringing Anne the water she had asked for. She let the tap run for some time, then rinsed a glass from the cupboard and filled it.

"We had to do some fast thinking," Joseph said. "We knew that our lives depended on getting as far away as possible. But how would we get away? We thought about buses and trains, but we couldn't be seen by anyone."

"I was afraid people might think we were two runaways," Anne said. "I felt I had to be the older sister, maybe even his mother. He may be a tall, slender young man now, but back then he was very small for his age and the cutest little boy you ever saw. He was the apple of my ma's eye."

Joseph grinned at everyone, his gorgeous eye sparkling with mischief.

"I hadn't worn makeup before, but I had watched my mother put it on for special occasions," she continued. "I had seen advertisements in magazines and admired the look. And of course I had never fussed with my hair like they did, so it was a real experiment. I had to look older in case a cop stopped us."

"She sure looked funny in Ma's makeup and her hair so different." Joseph smiled at his sister, respect and love written all over his face. "I remember laughing at her, thinking she looked like a clown. She wasn't too happy with me."

Jessica imaged what Anne might look like with bright red lips, heavy black mascara, and deep red rouge on her cheeks. She almost chuckled out loud.

"I didn't have time for jokes!" Anne said. "All that was on my mind was getting away. We kept to the back roads as much as possible. I didn't want to deal with heavy traffic, and I really wasn't familiar with highway driving."

"Where did you get your money?" Alex asked.

"Ma had saved some and given it to Marshall and me for a wedding present," she said. "And Larry had given her some money for safekeeping after he had decided to run away with us. I had saved money of my own too. Ma always gave me my share of the baby bonus, and I put it in the local bank. I made sure to bring the paperwork and records from Pa's desk, anything I thought we might need. We still had to be careful with money, though. We had lots of food, and in summertime we could eat at picnic tables and sleep in the truck."

Alex thought about a pair of toeless bright red high heels she had bought last month that cost two hundred and fifty dollars. She had loved them and just had to have them. She couldn't imagine what it would be like to be so careful with money. Hearing Anne and Joseph's story, giving up so much to make ends meet, made her feel guilty.

Ginny had been absorbed in the story, but suddenly her mind turned to shopping and the new skirt she had bought on her recent trip. She looked at Alex, thinking about how much they loved shopping. She hoped Phil would understand if they carried on seeing each other.

"Once I got onto the road at night, I found that I liked driving," Anne went on. "It really was peaceful. We found places to sleep during the day, and that worked fine. The parks along the highway north were wonderful. We were fascinated with all the places we had never heard of, places we had never been to."

Joseph nodded, smiling. "I'll never forget when we reached Parry Sound. We actually had supper in a diner and I had French fries. I was so excited! I had never eaten them before. I know how ridiculous that sounds, but we had never been to a restaurant. I wanted French fries all the time from then on. I drove Anne crazy. If ever we came to chip truck on the side of the road, she let me get some." He laughed. "On another stop, we had grilled cheese sandwiches!"

"As for coffee," Anne added, "I looked at the dark brown stuff and wanted to be so grown up, like every other woman there. Oh, we had coffee at home, but only Ma and Pa and our guests drank it. I put three of the little containers of milk in it, and I hate to say how much sugar. But I was determined that I was never going to be kid again."

Phil remembered his first taste of coffee when he was twelve years old. It had been when his mother had left her cup sitting on the table to go talk on the phone. He had sipped it—and it had tasted awful. Then he took another taste, and it was still terrible. He had gotten the sugar bowl and added three teaspoons, and it improved some, but not much. So he left it, and ten minutes later his mother came back, picked up the mug, and swallowed a good gulp. She had put it back on the table and stood looking at it. She'd sipped it again and quickly dumped it down the drain.

"We carried on until we came to Sudbury," Anne said. "It seemed like months had passed since we'd left, but of course it wasn't. I know something now that I didn't know then: the Lord was watching over us all the way."

"We stayed in Sudbury and Anne registered me in school," Joseph added. "We stayed one year, then moved on to Thunder Bay and did the same."

Jessica shook her head in disbelief that they'd had the strength to keep going. She doubted she would have been able to do it. But running for one's life made one capable of anything. She looked at them with deep, sorrowful eyes.

Anne continued her story. "I knew we couldn't stay in one place long, or we might be discovered. I had a goal in mind, and I wasn't going to let anything or anyone stop me. So we always had to move. We still weren't far enough away, and I was worried that the judge might find us."

"I have to tell you about one day I will never forget," Joseph said. "When we drove into a motel parking lot in Winnipeg, she turned to me and said, 'Joey, we're home. You can stay here as long as you like.'" He beamed at his sister. "It took us three weeks and a few days to find a small furnished apartment with a pullout couch. That was the best we could afford until she got a job. She registered me in high school, and then went through paper after paper looking for work. She landed the weirdest job you can imagine, working in the cafeteria of a Christian school. The pay was good, though.

"She even registered herself for college courses at night. She worked every day and got a second job on the weekend to save money for me to go to university. I took on delivering news-papers in two areas of the city to help with the expenses. And her drive to achieve a good education and make something of ourselves rubbed off on me. Sometimes we were ready to call it quits, but then the Lord came into it and we would buck up and carry on.

"We were drawn to a church affiliated with the school where Anne worked, and we were both were saved at the same time. We went forward and gave our lives to the Lord Jesus and never looked back." He paused. "Once we've been cleared of killing our family, we'll go home to continue our lives."

Joseph raised his eyes and looked at the rest of the people around them.

"Excuse me, Chief," he said after a moment. "I don't know if my sister sees what I do, but when I look at the lady next to you, I see my sister Rachel." Joseph addressed his question to the woman. "Do you mind if I ask, who you are? And where do you fit into this picture?"

Anne had been wondering the same thing.

Lorne smiled and turned to Alex. "Would you like to tell them who you are?"

"Yes, but I don't think you'll like it," Alex said to her young cousins. "Your mother was—"

"Hold it a minute," Jessica interrupted her. "I think this part is for me to tell." She looked at her niece and nephew. "You see, your mother was my sister. For fifteen years, I have waited to learn what happened in this house. I honestly hoped one day she would come back. I never dreamed it would be either of you. I'm glad you're all right. Your father took you all away from us. I tried everything to see you, but he kept us away. He said we were harassing your family, and I lived for the day when he might change his mind. So when all this happened... well, you must know what a burden it's put on us. I have to be honest with you. I know how unhappy your mother was. I know your father had gone weird. I felt he was keeping you all prisoners of a sort, and certainly brainwashing you. That's why we became strangers to you.

"I am ashamed to say that at times I thought your mother may have killed your father and run away with the rest of you. When we found the house all boarded up, we thought that Allen had gone to find you and bring you back. It never occurred to me that an outsider had murdered the family. I didn't know anything about the graves." Jessica put her arm around her daughter's shoulder.

"Alex is my daughter and a fine reporter. She helped bring the truth to light."

"Excuse me," a new voice said, breaking into the conversation.

Everyone turned to see a man enter the sunroom.

"When I told the officer at the door who I was, he let me quietly slip in," he said, turning to address Anne and Joseph. "I'm Stanley Rutherford, and the lady you're talking to is my wife, your Aunt Jessie. I'm afraid I played a part in all this. Jessie, when I tell you what I've done, please remember that I love you dearly with all my heart."

Stanley told them the story of how he had discovered the graves in the Canborough cemetery after Jess had sent him there to research their family history.

"When I found those graves, I knew one thing for sure: the family was dead, and they hadn't simply moved away," he finished.

Jessica looked at him in shock, hardly able to believe that he said nothing to her after all this time.

Joseph smiled at Anne. The siblings each knew what the other was thinking. Their memories had taken them back in time. Suddenly it seemed like yesterday when they'd sat in the grass and constructed those seven crosses from tree branches.

"Jess, I didn't tell you because I didn't yet know the whole truth," Stanley said to his wife. "I knew I had to do something more than just dig up a bunch of graves, and that's when I decided our daughter was the answer. She had skills at her disposal none of us had. She could find out what had happened and give us closure." He hesitated. "I knew about your theories, Jess, and I was afraid of what Alex would find out. But we needed to find out the truth."

Alex's eyes shifted to Joseph. A sense of peace seemed to be written on his face.

Stanley turned to his daughter. "I sent you the letter because I knew you wouldn't be able to resist it. I knew the family thing would get you. I realized later, after I had written the letter, that all I ever wanted was to give your mother peace of mind, and that the sister she loved hadn't done anything wrong. I'm sorry, dear. You've won awards for your journalism and we're very proud of you."

Jessie walked closer to her niece and nephew. "I'm glad you have come back, and I'm sure Chief Merritt can see now that you didn't kill your family." She put her arms around them. "I'm so sorry for what you've gone through. As awful as it is to say you, though, you've both done better than you would have if you'd stayed home and none of this had happened. I know your mother would be so proud of you." A single tear slid down her face. She tried to hold back her need to let go, or more tears would follow.

"If you're wondering who the sixth and seventh people in the graves were, they're Keith and Larry," Anne clarified. "I can't imagine a man, a judge, killing his own son because he was gay. I'm curious, Chief. Did his father ever report him missing?"

Lorne shook his head. "No. When we visited a few days ago, Judge Strandell made up a story."

"My pa did kill Marshall, though," Anne said sadly. "I'll agree with you, Aunt Jessie. There was something wrong with Pa's brain."

"Both Anne and I have relationships back home in Winnipeg," Joseph said. "In fact, I'm engaged to a wonderful girl. We haven't set a date yet, but in a couple of years we will get married. Anne is going to be married on Thanksgiving. We're both very happy and love our lives in Winnipeg."

Jessica smiled at them. "I hope you'll give my family a chance to get to know you now, even if it's only for a while. Will you come to our home? I'll get everyone together and we'll have a party just for you. I know it won't make up for the years you've been away, but you do have family that wants to love you."

Lorne stepped in back in the conversation. "However, I do need you to go with my detective back to the station and give your statements. Now that we know what happened, I'll get a warrant for the judge's arrest. If he happens to know you two have returned, and it wouldn't surprise me if he does, he'll be ready for us. I'm sure the last thing he wants is to go to prison, where he has sent many a person. I'm not sure what he might do. But I promise you he will pay for the deaths of your parents and siblings." He turned to look at Alex, who was standing to his right. "I can't take you with me for the arrest. I'll see that you get the whole story. You more than deserve it. One of my officers will take you back to my place."

"Okay," Alex said. She was of two minds, anxious to be involved but not sure if she wanted to witness the outcome firsthand. "I'm a reporter, Lorne, and I have to be there. I will stay out of the way, but I need the climax to my story."

Lorne nodded, not surprised. He would have to get used to Alex's job. She would never give it up, and he wouldn't want her to.

* * *

Half an hour later, Lorne and his crew pulled up in front of the judge's house. They got out and circled the property, not sure what to expect. They were working on the assumption that Judge Strandell knew they would be coming for him. After all, too many people knew the bodies had been found. Lorne worried that the judge might try to shoot his way out, to make an easy end to it.

Lorne and Phil, along with two armed officers, made their way to the front door. Lorne put his hand on the knob, expecting it to be locked. He was surprised that it wasn't.

"This isn't a good sign, guys," he said softly. Then, in a loud voice, he called, "Judge Strandell, it's the police. You are under arrest for the murder of the Williams family. Come out with your hands on the back of your head."

They waited, and there was no movement or sound.

"Judge Strandell!" he called again, repeating the command. When they still got no response, he nodded to Phil. "Okay, guys, let's go in."

Phil kicked the door down and it hit the wall with a bang. They entered in single file, keeping flat to the wall with their guns raised in case of trouble.

They quickly moved along the hall, each officer dispersing to different rooms. Still there was no sound.

Then, one by one, the word "Clear!" echoed throughout the house.

"Woman dead in the family room at the back of the house," someone called.

Lorne and Phil kept moving until they came to an open door. Phil peeked inside and stopped cold.

"Lorne, you need to see this."

Lorne walked into the room while Phil stood at the doorway with another couple of officers.

The chief walked over to the desk to find the judge slumped down in his chair. It was obvious that he had put the gun to his head. It was a gruesome sight, but not the first Lorne had seen over the years. A bottle was tipped on the desk, a little of its contents having spilled out. A bit of the drink was still in the glass on the blotter.

"Phil, call the coroner." Lorne left the room, making his way along the hall to where a couple of other officers stood by the back family room. The two large glass doors to the deck were swung wide open.

"I left the doors open," an officer said.

Lorne nodded. "Good thing."

He walked to the woman whose body lay on the floor, then stooped down to have a better look at what had happened. She had been shot in the head at close range.

"Phil is calling the coroner," Lorne said. "Stay here until he arrives to takes the body. Make sure the cameraman gets all the pictures we're going to need. Then get your gear. We have work to do." He paused, then added, "The judge is very well known, so make sure no reporters get near the place."

Lorne could make several guesses why the man had killed his wife. From the way position of the body, it seemed she had been standing when he did it. Yet there was no sign of horror on her face. He shook his head, questioning that.

He smiled to himself when he remembered his promise to Alex.

Never mind, he thought. *I'll make sure she gets the ending to her story.*

EPILOGUE

Two weeks later, a large funeral was held for the Williams family. It turned out to be a reunion of sorts, with years of hostilities and hurt feelings finally being resolved. The victims were finally laid to rest, in the same part of the cemetery, but this time with a proper burial and a long tombstone reflecting each person's name.

Alex and Lorne were married six months later at a huge wedding in Niagara-on-the-Lake Church. Phil was the best man and Ginny the matron of honor. The highlight of the wedding was Spider, who stood at the front of the church with Lorne and watched Alex walk down the aisle on her father's arm.

Afterward, a reception was held in a hotel overlooking the falls.

The men who worked for the judge, who were also involved in his crimes, were convicted for the parts they had played.

"God has a great sense of humor," Alex said to Lorne one day as they were settling into their lives together. "Everything went exactly as God knew it would."

ABOUT THE AUTHOR

I am married and widowed with two sons, one daughter, and several grandchildren. At the age of twenty, I went to work for the Toronto Telegram Publishing Company for several years and left when I got married. I then wrote for the local newspaper in the area where we moved.

I have always had a very imaginative mind and loved to write. Over the years, as computers became accessible in our homes, my husband, who was with IBM, bought me my first computer and the old Smith Corona was thrown out. The company moved us many times all over Canada, and some places in the U.S. for short periods of time. Many of my stories take place in these different towns or cities, although some names have been changed.

I have written Sunday school material that has been used by churches over the years. I have also written three Christmas plays, as well as Easter plays that were put on by adults several years ago.

I continued writing, but only after my husband's bout with cancer and his passing did I have time to take my writing seriously and begin to focus on mystery novels. All my stories have surprise endings, a little romance, a laugh or two, and even the odd tear that takes you right into the story.

In my spare time, I love to paint landscapes. My brushes, loaded with oil paint, add texture, helping my pictures to come alive.

SALLY CAMERON MYSTERIES - BOOK 1

A Holiday Weekend
& MURDER

SHIRLEY GLOSTER

OTHER BOOKS BY SHIRLEY GLOSTER

A Holiday Weekend and Murder
ISBN: 978-1-4866-1498-1

Sally Cameron, a smart and attractive criminal attorney, plans to spend a much-needed holiday weekend with her sister and brother-in-law at their country estate. But when she arrives late Friday evening, she finds many unanswered questions waiting for her.

First, her sister and brother-in-law are missing. Second, she hears a foreboding noise in the night, leaving her to believe someone is up to no good. Third, she discovers a jogging trail behind the house she knew nothing about.

Finally, in desperation, she goes back to the city seeking the help of a dear friend, Detective Joan Troon. Together they return to the estate only to discover an old farmhouse and a mysterious license plate. Soon Sally finds herself entangled in a dangerous police chase and the prisoner of a wanted man.

Be on the lookout for the next two books in the Sally Cameron Mysteries Series:

Book 2: *Secrets of the Past & Murder*
Book 3: *The Nightmare & Murder*